For more than forty years,
Yearling has been the leading name
in classic and award-winning literature
for young readers.

Yearling books feature children's
favorite authors and characters,
providing dynamic stories of adventure,
humor, history, mystery, and fantasy.

Trust Yearling paperbacks to entertain,
inspire, and promote the love of reading
in all children.

**Read all about The Saddle Club's adventures
in these great books!**

HORSE CRAZY

HORSE SHY

HORSE SENSE

HORSE POWER

TRAIL MATES

DUDE RANCH

HORSE PLAY

HORSE SHOW

HOOF BEAT

RIDING CAMP

Horse Play

Bonnie Bryant

A YEARLING BOOK

Published by Yearling, an imprint of Random House Children's Books
a division of Random House, Inc., New York

Yearling and the jumping horse design are registered trademarks of Random House, Inc.

"The Saddle Club" is a registered trademark of Bonnie Bryant Hiller.

"USPC" and "Pony Club" are registered trademarks of the United States Pony Clubs, Inc., at The Kentucky Horse Park, 4071 Iron Works Pike, Lexington, KY 40511-8462.

Visit us on the Web! www.randomhouse.com/kids

Educators and librarians, for a variety of teaching tools, visit us at
www.randomhouse.com/teachers

ISBN: 978-0-553-15754-3 (pbk.)—ISBN: 978-0-385-90423-0 (lib. bdg.)

Printed in the United States of America

Originally published by Bantam Skylark in 1989

First Yearling Edition September 2007

20 19 18 17 16 15 14 13 12 11

For my horse-crazy sister, Molly Bryant

"I THINK IT'S the silly season," Stevie Lake announced to her two best friends as the three of them dressed for their riding class. Stevie's blue eyes sparkled mischievously. She swept her shoulder-length, dark blond hair back from her face.

"What do you mean?" Carole Hanson asked as she pulled her curly black hair into a ponytail that would fit under her riding hat.

"Did you hear what happened to Max?" Stevie asked instead. "Max" was Max Regnery, their riding instructor and the owner of Pine Hollow Stables.

"What?" Lisa Atwood asked with concern. Lisa, a year

older than Stevie and Carole, was inclined to be more serious than Stevie. Stevie readily admitted, though, that almost everybody in the world was inclined to be more serious than she was!

"Well," Stevie began, putting one booted foot on the bench and leaning toward her friends. "It seems that Max has lost a student." Stevie began giggling.

Carole and Lisa could never resist Stevie's giggles. They joined in, too, even before they heard the funny part.

"See, this man named Mr. Small wanted a private lesson. Max asked the new stableboy, Jesse, to saddle Small a horse. Jesse thought Max told him to saddle a small horse. So he saddled the pony, Nickel! Mr. Small, is anything *but* small. He climbed on Nickel, and his feet almost touched the ground! It turns out he's really sensitive about being so tall—doesn't like jokes about his name—and thought the stableboy was making fun of him. The man's face turned all red and he blew up at Max. He stormed out, saying he'd never ride here again."

"Poor Max," Carole said between giggles as she tugged on her breeches and began to pull on her high riding boots. Carole was the most experienced rider of the trio, but they all loved horses and had even formed their own horse-crazy group called The Saddle Club. Carole, daughter of a Marine Corps colonel, had been riding since she was a very little girl on Marine Corps bases. When her family had settled in Willow Creek, Virginia, a few years ago, she'd begun studying at Pine Hollow. Several championship riders, and even some Olympic riders, had studied with Max, or his father, or his grandfather. Carole hoped, one day, to be one of Max's champion graduates. "But Max is so nice. He'd never make fun of a new rider—even though *some* of the people who come here . . ." Her words trailed off as she rolled her eyes.

Lisa and Stevie laughed. "Remember that guy who came all decked out in hunting duds, red coat and everything?" Stevie sat cross-legged on the bench.

"The one who didn't know one end of a horse from another," Lisa said, nodding. "He only lasted one day here."

"And then there was my brother," Stevie said, shaking her head with a disgusted look. Stevie's older brother, Chad, had decided to take up riding when he'd gotten a crush on Lisa. It turned out that his attempts at riding weren't much more successful than his romance. Each had only lasted a few weeks.

"He wasn't so bad, Stevie," Lisa said, grinning.

"Yeah, and at least he stuck around long enough to be helpful at the gymkhana," Carole said. "Not like these people who spend zillions of dollars on fancy clothes, without realizing that the horses don't care what they wear!"

"Ahem," Lisa said. It was a way of reminding Carole that Lisa always wore proper riding clothes. It wasn't so much *Lisa* who cared about how she dressed. Her *mother* cared a lot about such things and saw to it that Lisa was properly dressed for riding—and everything else. "And speaking of that," Lisa continued, "you may have noticed this box." She patted the carton on the bench next to her. Her friends noticed the package for the first time.

"So?" Stevie said, curiosity aroused.

"It's a new pair of riding pants. My mother's aunt, Aunt Maude, is visiting us. She brought me this as a present. I haven't even opened it yet. She's coming with mother to watch the class today and will expect to see me in them."

"That's really nice," Carole said. "I wish I had a great-aunt who'd give me clothes like that."

"You don't know what you're wishing for," Lisa said ominously. "One time she brought me some pajamas. Only she'd bought them in the boys' department!" With that, she began to open the box, which bore the mark of a very fancy department store at a nearby mall. "There was another time she brought me a—oh, look at these!"

Lisa held up an expensive pair of fawn-colored riding breeches.

"Nice," Stevie said admiringly. Though she generally preferred to wear jeans when she rode, she knew good riding clothes when she saw them.

Lisa held them up to her waist and turned to show them off to Carole, who stood by the old mirror, tucking in her shirttails.

"They are nice—but there's one little problem, Lisa, don't you think?" Carole remarked with a grin.

Lisa looked down. The pants looked just fine to her. Puzzled, she turned back to Carole. "I don't see any problem," she said.

"Maybe not—if your boots have grown overnight!"

Lisa gasped, looking down at the pants again. Carole was right. Dear Aunt Maude had bought her a pair of breeches—pants that stopped just below the knees. They were meant to be worn with high boots like the ones Carole had just put on. Unfortunately, Lisa usually wore jodhpurs—pants that came down to a rider's ankles— which were worn with boots that came just above the ankles. *That* was the kind of boots that Lisa had in her cubby. There was no way she could wear short pants and short boots. There would be a whole lot of bare leg between them.

"Oh, no," she said. "And I *told* Aunt Maude what kind of pants I wear!" she added, distressed. But then she caught the look on Stevie's face and the one on Carole's. Simultaneously, all three girls exploded into giggles.

"Aunt Maude is going to love the look!" Stevie said.

"Sure, and next thing you know, Veronica diAngelo will want to copy it!" Carole added. Stevie and Lisa laughed loudly. Veronica was the snobby daughter of Willow Creek's wealthiest banker. Although she was a pretty good rider, she was always much more concerned with how she looked than how she rode.

Just for fun, Lisa slipped into her new riding pants and pulled on her boots, leaving a long white gap of bare leg between the top of one and the bottom of the other. She paraded to the dingy mirror, imitating a fashion model.

"Zee new look ziss year . . ." Stevie said, grabbing a riding whip and holding its grip to her mouth as if it were a microphone and she were the emcee at a fashion show. Carole sat down on the bench, pretending to be the audience.

"Oooooh," she said. Lisa twirled. "Aaaaah!" Carole responded.

"And ziss outfit can be parfaitly completed by zee t-shirt and zee jacquette of bright peenk!"

"Definitely the silly season," Carole said, trying to control her giggles.

Lisa stopped short. "But just what am I going to wear in class? I can't ride like this!" she said, the sensible Lisa once again.

"No, you're right," Carole agreed. "You can't. And you don't have time to go home and change, either." Carole tapped her index finger against her chin. "I know!" she announced, her eyes lighting up. "Chaps. I think Mrs. Reg keeps a pair in her office. I'm sure she'll let you borrow them."

"Great idea," Stevie added. "I'll get them for you. That'll cover your legs."

"And my new pants. Aunt Maude will never understand."

"From what you say, she won't understand anyway, so you haven't lost anything!" Stevie quipped over her shoulder as she headed off to find Max's mother. Mrs. Reg served as equipment manager for the stable as well as confidante for the Saddle Club members.

When Stevie returned, Lisa put on the chaps and zipped them up. They were like suede leggings, designed to be worn over pants. Usually riders wore chaps for extra warmth, protection from scraggly bushes, or to help grip the horse better, since the suede was less likely to slip on a leather saddle than denim, cotton, or synthetics. Although the chaps felt a little odd over Lisa's bare calves, they did the trick. All that showed of Aunt Maude's breeches was the seat, but Lisa didn't have time to worry about that. Class was about to start!

TEN MINUTES LATER, they were ready for class, and so were their horses. The girls each touched the stable's "good-luck horseshoe" and mounted their horses.

Stevie moved her horse into line and looked around at her classmates. She was a friendly girl and got along with almost everybody. The *almost* was to make an exception in the case of one Veronica diAngelo, who sat there, as usual, with a smug look on her face.

"The problem with Veronica is that she doesn't just *think* she's better than everybody else. She *knows* she is," Stevie whispered to Lisa, who nodded in response.

Stevie was riding a horse named Comanche. She usually rode him, because they were such a good match. He was a chestnut gelding with an independent streak just like Stevie's. Today he was acting up a bit, tossing his head and taking steps backwards.

Stevie shortened the reins in response, then leaned forward. "Hey, Comanche," she said, "remember me? I'm the one who's in charge here." She patted his neck reassuringly, but the tone of her voice and the firmness of her hand on the reins could leave no doubt in the horse's mind about who was the boss. He shifted his weight easily and relaxed. Stevie knew that most horses made a habit of testing their riders. It was important to let the horse know who was in charge.

"We're going to play a game today," Max announced. "I want to see how much control you have over your horses." Stevie shifted her weight deeper in the saddle and Comanche glanced back over his shoulder at her.

"It's called 'Break and Out,'" Max told the riders. Stevie liked this game. The idea was that Max would call a gait—walk, trot, or canter—and the riders had two strides to get their horses to the new gait. If they didn't get the horse into the new gait or if the horse broke gait, they were out, sort of like musical chairs.

"Walk," he announced. Stevie got Comanche walking. The other riders did the same. This game was always easy at the beginning. The horses marched in a circle around the ring.

"Trot!" Max said. Stevie's calves gripped Comanche's

side firmly and he broke into a trot immediately. Betsy Cavanaugh wasn't so fast. Her horse kept plodding along. Max pointed to the edge of the ring. Betsy was out.

Stevie could see Veronica sitting up straight, ready for the next change. The logical gait was a canter now and it was clear to Stevie that Veronica was ready for it.

Max raised his hand to get their attention before announcing the next gait. Before he spoke, Veronica had already signaled to her horse, Barq, for a canter. He broke out of the pack and began a rocking canter around the ring.

"Walk!" Max announced.

Veronica's face turned a bright red. In somebody else, that might be from embarrassment. But in Veronica, it was fury.

"How *could* you?" she demanded of Max, reining Barq down to a walk and guiding him over to Max, who simply pointed to the edge of the ring where Betsy waited patiently.

Stevie and Comanche were walking next to Carole, on Diablo. They both watched Veronica in amusement.

"See," Stevie whispered. "I told you—" she began.

"Trot!" Max said. Comanche and Diablo followed instructions. It made it harder for Stevie to talk to Carole, but it wasn't going to stop her.

"I told you," she said louder. Comanche was trotting very quickly. He pulled ahead of Diablo. Stevie had to look over her shoulder at Carole to finish her thought.

"I told you it was the silly season!" she said, but she practically had to yell it. Not only did Carole hear her, and Lisa, but everybody else in the class, including Veronica. The girl's face was stony and bright red when Stevie looked at her. She spoke to Stevie silently, but her words were clear as she mouthed them. "I'll get you for that!" Veronica said.

"Canter!" Max said. Stevie touched Comanche behind his girth with her left heel and the horse began cantering. Stevie loved the wonderful rocking feel of Comanche's canter. It made her forget everything else.

AFTER CLASS, STEVIE removed Comanche's tack and gave him a good grooming. One of Pine Hollow's many traditions was that each student was responsible for his or her own horse, grooming included. As Comanche munched away at the fresh hay she'd supplied, Stevie used a curry comb to bring a sheen to his auburn coat. By having the students take care of the horses, Pine Hollow was able to keep its costs down, and that was something everybody could appreciate. Right then, however, Stevie wished there were a gigantic staff of grooms to take over the work. It was a hot afternoon and she'd rather be in her own pool than in Comanche's stall.

"Come on, boy," she said, trying to convince Comanche to step to the right so she could get around him. She patted his rump. He didn't move. She reached to scratch him under his jaw. His mouth sprung open as if he were talking. She looked at him in surprise.

"Did you say something, boy?" she asked with a giggle.

She scratched him again. His jaw began to move again. Stevie dropped her own voice and spoke for Comanche as his mouth opened and closed. "Lay off the talk, sister. Just give me some peace and quiet so I can eat my hay." The horse regarded her curiously. Stevie giggled.

She'd always wondered what a horse would say if he could speak. Now she'd found she could speak for him! It was fun.

"You going to give me trouble?" she asked.

Then she began scratching his chin and as soon as his jaw opened, she dropped her voice and spoke for him. "Me give *you* trouble? What do you think you were giving me all through the class?"

"I was just doing what Max told me to do!" Stevie defended herself.

"Teacher's pet!" Comanche responded in a taunting voice.

Stevie scrunched up her eyebrows to think. "No, I think *you're* the teacher's pet," she remarked, then smiled at her own joke. Comanche leaned forward to munch on some hay. Stevie shoved his hindquarters a bit to get him to move over so she could return to the grooming.

Stevie began working on his left side. Comanche stepped back to the left, boxing her in. She growled at the horse, but he calmly munched on his hay. Stevie was about to start him talking again when Carole's voice came over the horse's neck.

"Stevie, you there?" Carole asked. She was standing at the door to the stall.

"Unfortunately," Stevie said from behind Comanche's haunches. "It's so hot—I bet even Comanche would rather be in my swimming pool."

"That would be a sight to see," Carole said, laughing. "Maybe this will help—here's your soda." Carole perched the can on the ledge by the door of the stall, just within Stevie's reach. At the end of every class at Pine Hollow, one of the riders was assigned to get sodas for all the other riders. Carole had the honors today.

"Thanks," Stevie said.

Carole watched for a second. All she could see was a hand reach out from under Comanche's neck, circle the can, and disappear with it.

There was a long silence.

"Wonderful," Stevie said. The can reappeared on the ledge.

"See you later," Carole said.

"Wait—don't go. I want to ask you something."

"Well, okay, but I've still got to untack Diablo."

"I'll help you when I'm done here," Stevie promised. "But I was just thinking about something—"

Stevie paused. Carole knew she was collecting her thoughts, and would start talking in a second. In the meantime, since Stevie was totally invisible on the far side of the large chestnut horse, Carole had the eerie feeling she was actually having a conversation with Comanche. He looked at her balefully, munching on his hay.

"Remember our drill classes?" Stevie asked Carole.

"Sure," she said. The Saddle Club had been working on drills with Max for a while during the summer camp session. They'd all enjoyed the difficult work and the precision it required tremendously, but the classes had stopped when the month of camp ended.

"Why don't we see if Max will start them again? It really was neat, even with just the three of us. Maybe now other people would want to get in on it, too, don't you think?"

Carole's eyes lit up. "That's a great idea!" she said enthusiastically.

"Why don't you ask Max, then?" Stevie suggested.

"Your idea, you get to ask him," Carole replied. "Besides," Carole continued, "Max has been sort of cranky lately and you have a way of talking people into things— even cranky people. *And*, I have to finish delivering sodas and then untack Diablo and groom him."

"I said I'd help," Stevie reminded her.

"*After* you ask Max," Carole said. "See you," she added with a laugh.

Stevie began to tell Carole that she was a much more convincing person and Max would be more likely to go along with Carole's suggestion, but she realized, when she was about four sentences into her argument, that Carole had disappeared. Comanche, now clean and shiny, content with his hay, just nudged his empty water bucket in response.

"See how convincing I am?" she said to him. "I couldn't even convince Carole to convince Max!"

She unhooked the bucket and took it to the faucet, then rinsed it carefully. When Stevie was certain the bucket was clean, she put some cool water in it and brought it back to Comanche's stall. She hooked the bucket on his wall so he could reach it. He began drinking right away.

"I'm even being ignored by a horse," she grumbled. It was time to talk to Max.

Max's office was in the main house on the far side of the indoor ring. In fact, it overlooked the ring so that he could oversee classes taking place there. In nice weather, however, almost all riding was outdoors.

Stevie let herself into the main building and walked along the little hallway that led to Max's office. He was inside, talking animatedly on the telephone. The office door was ajar, but he was speaking so intently that Stevie felt she'd be intruding if she walked in. She stood outside his office and waited. Carole was right that Max had been cranky and out of sorts recently. He seemed ·distracted, too, as if he had a lot on his mind. Although Stevie didn't exactly want to snoop, Max was talking loudly and agitatedly on the phone. Stevie heard every word.

"But I can't do it now!" Max said, protesting loudly. "It's out of the question. . . . Yes, I know what that means. If I lose it, I lose it! Of course it will affect the stable and the riders will suffer, but they'll get used to it when the time comes."

Can't do it? Stevie said to herself. *Can't do what? Why will we suffer? What will we get used to?*

"Of *course* it's a matter of money!" Max said, raising his voice further. "If you want this business arrangement to work, you've just got to give me more time—or the whole deal will fall through and we'll be out of business altogether!"

Stevie jumped when Max slammed the phone into its cradle. Stevie wasn't sure exactly what she'd just heard, but two things were clear. First, this was no time to ask Max for a favor. Second, whatever was going on with Max, it was a job for The Saddle Club!

"BUT DEAR, AUNT Maude and I are here right now. We can take you home and you won't have to walk," Mrs. Atwood told Lisa as Carole and Stevie looked on. Lisa was more than a little embarrassed to be having this conversation with her mother in front of her friends, especially when Stevie had just told them that they absolutely had to have a Saddle Club meeting right away at TD's—their favorite ice cream place at the nearby shopping center.

"It's okay, Mom, I can walk home by myself," Lisa assured her mother.

"I can pick you up at the shopping center, dear," Mrs. Atwood persisted. "Or better still, why don't your friends come over to our house? I'm sure we've got plenty of ice cream and sauces there. You could have your snack right in our kitchen. . . ."

Snack, Lisa thought with annoyance. Her mother made it sound like milk and cookies after school. Why couldn't her mother recognize that she was almost grown up—almost fourteen?

"Mom," she said much more patiently than she felt, "we'll walk to TD's and I'll be home in about an hour. I'll see you and Aunt Maude at home."

"I don't get it," Lisa said after her mother walked away. "She always tries to treat me as if I were still a little girl."

I don't get it, either," Stevie said. "My mother was only too glad when she didn't have to drive me to and from riding lessons. But that's not the real mystery we have to solve this afternoon. Let's get dressed and over to TD's. Right away."

Carole and Lisa tried to get Stevie to tell them what was up before they left the stable, but Stevie only said that the walls had ears. The girls were dying of curiosity. What could be so important that it shouldn't be overheard by anybody?

The girls changed into their street clothes as quickly as possible and walked over to the town's shopping center.

It wasn't a mall by any definition. It was just a little shopping center with a supermarket, a jewelry store, a couple of shoe stores, a music store, and best of all, Tastee Delight.

"So?" Carole challenged Stevie when they were seated in TD's and had ordered their sundaes.

"I'm worried," Stevie began.

"We already know that," Lisa said sensibly. "But what exactly are you worried about?"

"Max." She had both of her friends' attention immediately. Stevie leaned forward on the table and spoke in hushed tones, repeating as much as she could remember of the conversation she'd overheard from outside Max's office. "It was like he was desperately trying to avoid paying something. And he was worried about the impact it would have on *us*!"

"This doesn't sound good," Carole said, her face clouded with concern.

Lisa regarded her two friends thoughtfully. She was trying to absorb everything Stevie was telling them, as well as the possible implications. While Lisa was thinking and Stevie and Carole were speculating, Veronica diAngelo sauntered into TD's, followed by her group of admirers. She always tried to have a few adoring friends who trailed her wherever she went.

"Look who's here," Stevie remarked, spotting Veronica. She wrinkled her nose.

"Oh—hello," Veronica said unenthusiastically, greeting The Saddle Club as if they weren't really good enough to be in the same restaurant with her.

The girls returned her greeting with equal enthusiasm. Veronica stuck her nose in the air and headed for her own table. She was so busy being snooty that she didn't see a TD's waitress, bearing whipped cream—covered sundaes. The two smashed right into one another and the waitress ended up dumping two sundaes all over Veronica.

It was a sight for sore eyes. Veronica was so angry, she just sputtered. "My outfit! Do you know what it *cost?*"

The waitress stood up and offered Veronica a hand. Although the collision had been one hundred percent Veronica's fault, the waitress tried to be nice about it. "I'll pay to have your clothes cleaned," she offered politely.

"You'll pay to replace them!" Veronica retorted rudely.

That was too much for Stevie, who knew that Veronica's father was a very wealthy banker. She went to the waitress's rescue. "Don't worry," she assured the woman. "Her daddy can afford to replace them."

Veronica glared at Stevie. Stevie tried to glare back, but the image of the impeccably groomed Veronica diAngelo sprawled on the floor of TD's wearing designer jeans and a caramel sundae was just too much. She began to laugh. And it only got worse when Carole and Lisa joined in on the laughter. There were even some smirks from Veronica's group.

"My daddy can afford to replace a *lot* of things," Veronica said threateningly, her anger now focused totally on Stevie. "In fact, he can buy anything in this town!" she announced. She shifted her weight and stood up, making no attempt to brush off the gooey mess on her outfit. She put her hands on her hips, faced Stevie squarely, and added, "If I say the word, he just might. And it would be too bad for you!"

With that, she turned and marched out of TD's. Her friends put on somber faces and followed after her.

The Saddle Club gave the waitress a hand cleaning up the mess Veronica had left and they returned to their table.

"Can you imagine what life would be like at TD's if Veronica's father owned it?" Lisa asked, frowning.

"I'd stop coming, wouldn't you?" Carole said to her friends. Lisa nodded, but Stevie was deep in thought. "Wouldn't *you*?" Carole asked again.

Stevie shook her head. "I don't think she was talking about Daddy buying *TD's*," she said. "I just put two and two together and got one big nightmare!"

"Oh, no!" Carole gasped, suddenly arriving at the same conclusion Stevie had just reached. "Do you think the person you heard Max talking to was Mr. diAngelo?"

Lisa paled. "You mean you think he may take over Pine Hollow?"

"You should have heard Max," Stevie said. "He was talking about money and expenses—and how he needed more time. Then, worst of all, he was talking about what it was going to mean to *us*—the riders. You talk about money with bankers—like Mr. diAngelo. And you sound so worried when you talk to them if they're going to do something terrible—like take over Pine Hollow!"

"We've got to *do* something!" Lisa said.

"Yeah, but what?" Carole asked.

Both girls looked to Stevie. She was the one who always 'had the bright ideas, the plans, the answers.

"We've got to save Pine Hollow for Max!" Stevie said with determination. "We've got to get him more money."

"Sure, but how?" Carole asked.

Stevie wrinkled her forehead and stared at the sundae the waitress had just put in front of her.

"Well, there are lots of things we can do," she began. Her friends waited expectantly. "First of all, we've got to get more students at the stable. As long as Max is giving lessons, there's money coming in, right?"

Carole and Lisa nodded.

"Then, we have to think how we can raise money for him—if only we can do it in time!"

"I think it's the end of the silly season," Carole added.

They all agreed to that.

3

"COME ON, LET'S pay up and get out of here!" Stevie said. Lisa wondered if maybe her boysenberry sundae on coffee ice cream hadn't been the success Stevie had been hoping for, but obviously that wasn't the case. Stevie gobbled the last few bites of it, scraped the dish clean and grabbed her check.

"What's our first step?" Lisa asked, trying to impose some logic and order on Stevie's frenetic activity.

"We have to find some new students for Max, that's our first step," she announced, standing up.

Lisa and Carole followed her. They each paid their checks then left TD's. Lisa glanced at her watch. Her mother would expect her home in about a half an hour. She hoped that Stevie's plan, whatever it was, wouldn't take more time than that today. Not that she minded staying with her friends longer, but her mother seemed so concerned with her these days. It made Lisa concerned about her mother.

"Look! There's a good candidate!" Stevie said, pointing to a policeman who was walking across the shopping center. Willow Creek was a pretty small town and everybody knew Officer Manchester. Stevie ran over to him.

"Uh, wait, Stevie," Carole began, but it was too late.

"What's the matter, Stephanie?" he asked. He always called all the young people in town by their formal names.

"Oh, nothing," she said, casually. "I just wanted to do you a favor," she replied. "I wanted to let you know about something really terrific over at Pine Hollow."

Officer Manchester cocked his head and seemed interested in what she had to say. Lisa didn't think it meant much. He was a good policeman, and a good policeman *always* listened carefully to people.

"Max is offering a special newcomers' package at the stable. Twelve lessons for the price of ten. It's such a deal you couldn't possibly miss out on it."

"Very interesting," the policeman said. "Twelve for the price of ten?"

"Only for newcomers," Stevie said.

Carole and Lisa glanced at each other. There was nothing new or special about this offer. It was the newcomers' package Max *always* offered.

"Sounds like a good deal to me," the policeman told Stevie. "I'll have to think about it."

"You do that," Stevie said. She sounded just like a salesman who was about to land a big deal. She reached out and shook Officer Manchester's hand. He shook her hand, saluted briefly, and continued on his rounds.

The girls began to walk in the opposite direction, toward the street where Lisa and Stevie's houses were.

"What made you think he'd be interested in beginner's lessons?" Carole asked Stevie when he was out of earshot.

"Oh, I don't know," Stevie said. "Just seemed sort of natural, a police officer and horses. With some people, you just get this feeling. . . ."

"Maybe it's because you've seen him on a horse before?" Carole suggested.

Stevie stopped. "I have?" she said, puzzled.

"Think about it," Carole said.

Stevie thought. As she thought, she could hear the familiar clop of a horse's hooves. The girls all turned around. There, mounted on one of the police department's horses, was Officer Manchester. Stevie realized that she was right to think that he and horses were a natural combination. In order to be a mounted policeman, he had to be an excellent rider already.

Almost anybody else would be embarrassed by the mistake, Lisa thought, especially since Officer Manchester had been wearing breeches and high boots when Stevie gave him her sales pitch for beginners. But Lisa and Carole watched in amazement as Stevie walked over to him again. He pulled his horse to a stop. She held the reins and patted the horse's nose while she chatted with him some more.

"What's she doing now?" Lisa asked Carole.

"I think she's telling him about the 'special' Max has for experienced riders."

"Ten lessons for the price of ten?" Lisa asked.

They were still laughing when Stevie returned.

Come on, I'll go talk to the man in Sights 'n' Sounds," Stevie said, pointing to the music store. "You two work on the shoe stores. Maybe if they sell riding boots there, they could get them at discount and save *twice* on their lessons!"

"You're crazy," Carole said. "Have you considered trying to sell freezers to Eskimos?"

Stevie shook her head thoughtfully. "No," she said. "But do you think they'd like riding lessons?"

A HALF AN hour later, Lisa was in a phone booth, calling her mother at Stevie's insistence, to explain why she was going to be late.

"Ask her if she wants to take lessons," Stevie hissed at Lisa. Lisa gave her a look.

"I think I got the assistant manager in Sights 'n' Sounds interested," Stevie told Carole while they waited. Lisa was having a hard time with her mother.

"I'll be home a little later, Mom," Lisa assured her. "I'll have your brownies then. I'll be *fine*. Don't worry about me, okay?"

"That's the silliest thing anybody ever said to Lisa's mother," Stevie remarked irreverently. Carole wouldn't have said it out loud, but she certainly agreed. Mrs. Atwood was a born worrier. Nothing would stop that.

Lisa hung up the phone and sighed. "What next?" she asked with resignation.

"The supermarket," Stevie announced.

"You think the butcher wants to ride?" Carole asked.

"Not the people who work there," Stevie said, rolling her eyes, "the shoppers."

"Well, *excuse* me," Carole quipped.

Stevie grinned, then explained.

"See, you can tell from what people put in their shopping carts if they've got kids in the house. So, we go up to somebody with a lot of cupcakes, frozen pizza, or canned spaghetti—stuff like that—and sell them on riding lessons for their kids. Isn't that a great idea?"

"It's pretty clever," Carole said. "But then, you always are pretty clever."

"You're right about that," Stevie agreed. "So let's go."

The girls walked into the supermarket with determination. Carole and Lisa followed Stevie as she wandered up and down the aisles, peering into shopping carts. She got a lot of dirty looks.

Stevie seemed to be looking for just exactly the right blend of peanut butter, potato chips, pizza, and soda. She began to move in on a likely candidate. Lisa and Carole hid behind a large display of paper towels. They wanted to hear Stevie's sales pitch.

"Excuse me," Stevie said to the tired-looking woman who was pushing a cart filled with frozen foods and desserts. "Would you be interested in starting your children on a new and wonderful activity? One which will hold their interest, provide healthful exercise, teach them responsibility . . . ?" She paused to let her message sink in.

The woman looked at her briefly and then, reaching for some fruit-flavored juice, said "No." She turned her cart around and walked away from Stevie.

"It figures," Stevie said to Carole and Lisa when they emerged from behind the paper towels. "Did you see all the junk she was buying for her kids? She doesn't care about them at all!"

"Actually," Lisa said, glancing at the departing customer, "judging from her weight and everything, I bet that all that junk is for her and she doesn't have any kids."

"Good news for them," Stevie said, then wrinkled her brows comically.

Lisa wasn't sure that made sense, but before she could figure it out, they were completely surrounded by little girls in brown uniforms. A determined but haggard woman was trying to control them.

"Now, girls," she said. "if we're going to make our picnic, we must choose our ingredients carefully. I don't want to see anything in the cart that's not on the list. Amy, put back that bag of candy! Elsa, why are you taking the small package of rice when you know there are fifteen of us?" She spoke so quickly to the unruly group that it all sounded as if it were one sentence.

Stevie eyed her friends. "You get the list and stick with the kids. I'll do the sales pitch," she said.

Lisa and Carole swung into action. The first thing they had to do was to stop one of the little girls from using their cart as a weapon to ram unsuspecting customers. Carole grabbed the front and stopped it just in the nick of time, before it upset a young mother with two toddlers clinging to the sides of their own cart.

Lisa glanced at the shopping list, clutched by one of the scouts, scribbled out in nearly illegible elementary school handwriting.

She squinted at it. "Five pounds of rice," she decoded. "First one of you to find the package gets to ride on the back of the cart!"

The girls shouted with glee at the challenge and soon cleared the aisles, leaving Stevie to do her thing.

"Imagine how much they'd all enjoy riding lessons," Stevie said to the Scout leader. "And how much they'd learn about responsibility and caring. And how easy it would be for you to just sit and watch while the stable owner, Max Regnery, does all the work."

"What's the phone number?" the woman asked. Stevie hastily scribbled it for her.

Convincing the Scout leader turned out to be a whole lot easier than helping the little girls finish their shopping. It took Lisa and Carole another half hour to round up the ingredients on the list—and fifteen minutes after that to round up all the Scouts.

"Poor checkout lady," Stevie remarked, watching the girls pile their purchases on the counter. One of the girls was trying to ride on the conveyor belt.

"More to the point, poor Max," Carole said.

"I've got to go now," Lisa said. "You want to come over to my house for a while? My mom's made some brownies. . . ."

"I don't think I could look at another brownie for at least a week," Carole said, "in or out of uniform!"

"I know what you mean," Lisa said, "but there's no escape for me. I've got to get home now."

"Me, too," Carole said. "Here comes my bus. What about you, Stevie?"

"I have a few more ideas I'd like to try," Stevie said, rather mysteriously. "I'll see you on Wednesday at the next class."

They waved to each other and went their separate ways.

4

ON WEDNESDAY, WHEN it was time to leave for her next riding class, Lisa sneaked out the front door of her house. Her mother was in the kitchen, and Lisa was sure if she showed her face, her mother would insist on driving her over to the stable. Lisa didn't want her mother to drive her. She liked to walk; besides, she might run into Stevie, and they could walk together. Stevie's mother almost never drove her over to the stable. She never even offered to drive her. Stevie was lucky.

"Hey, there!" Stevie greeted her at the corner of their street.

"You sound awfully cheerful," Lisa remarked. "What's up?"

"Business," Stevie said. "I think we're about to see a remarkable surge in business at Pine Hollow."

"What have you done?" Lisa asked.

"Oh, I made a few phone calls. Talked to some people," Stevie said casually. "I think Max will be pleased."

"Enough to save Pine Hollow?" Lisa asked.

"I don't know," Stevie told her frankly as they walked along the field that bordered the road to the stable. "I don't know how much money Max needs, but I'm pretty sure he's going to have some new students."

"Great!" Lisa said. "You're really terrific, Stevie, you know?"

Stevie smiled proudly.

"I mean it," Lisa assured her. Stevie already believed it. "A lot of people wouldn't have the vaguest idea what to do in a crisis like this. You *always* know what to do. Max is going to be so happy."

"Oh, but we can't tell him. . . ."

"He's going to find out," Lisa said. "Don't you think?"

"Not from me, you, or Carole," she said. "See, The Saddle Club is sort of like the Lone Ranger. We do good, but we have to do it anonymously."

"Maybe more like Robin Hood," Lisa suggested. "Veronica is sort of the Sheriff of Nottingham. Her father is the greedy Prince John."

"And I'm Maid Marian!"

Lisa shook her head. "No, you're Robin Hood, remember?"

"I remember," Stevie said. "Sometimes, though, I'd like to be the damsel in distress, you know?"

Lisa regarded her friend carefully. "No way," she told Stevie. "There's nothing helpless about you. You can't even fake the part."

Stevie shrugged. "I guess you're right. I'd never had made it in those days. It would have been a total waste of a good coat if Sir Walter Raleigh had laid his jacket across a puddle for me. I'd just back up a bit, run for it, and leap the puddle by myself."

"Yes, I know," Lisa said. "That's exactly what you'd do." She smiled, thinking about Stevie's independence and individuality. It was one of the things Lisa liked about Stevie.

A car was pulling into the stable's driveway as the girls walked up to the door. The window rolled down. "Yoo hoo, Stevie!" the driver called. Lisa sort of recognized the woman's voice, but she wasn't sure how. She turned to look.

"Hi!" Stevie cried out with delight. Lisa saw that the driver of the car was the waitress from TD's.

"Thanks for the tip," she said to Stevie.

"What tip?" Lisa asked Stevie.

"The tip that she should try riding lessons," Stevie said with a wink.

•   •   •

"THEN I TOOK my little brother's homeroom address list,"
Stevie said to Carole and Lisa as the three of them were
dressing for class. "I called all the mothers of all the girls
and told them about Pine Hollow. Three of them said
they'd definitely sign their daughters up for lessons." Stevie tucked her blouse into her pants and smiled impishly.
"I'm something, aren't I?" she asked, reaching into the
deep recesses of her cubby for her boots.

"You certainly are, and the question is *what*," Carole
teased. She pulled on one boot, but it didn't seem right.
She looked down at her feet, puzzled.

"Something wrong?" Lisa asked.

"I think so," Carole said. "But I'm not sure what." She
tugged harder. The boot wouldn't go on.

"Maybe your feet got swollen in the hot weather?" Lisa
suggested.

"Maybe," Carole said, tugging even harder.

Lisa reached for her boots. The right boot went on just
fine, but when she got to her left boot, she knew something was definitely wrong. Her foot slipped into it and
then slid around on the bottom.

"We must have gotten our boots mixed up," Lisa said,
solving the mystery. "I've got one of yours; you've got one
of mine."

Carole nodded and the girls exchanged boots.

"Now I feel like Cinderella," Lisa said, slipping on her
other boot. It fit just right.

"You two!" Stevie said, teasing her friends. "You're the

neat ones. I'm the slob. How could you mix up your boots?"

"Well, we all know who the practical joker is in this place, don't we?" Carole said, glancing at Stevie, who was famous for such things.

"Not me," Stevie said as she began pulling on her own boots. Then, almost as if it were proof of her innocence, Stevie found that her boots were filled to the bootstraps with oats!

"What's this?" she asked furiously. "Did you two do this to me and cover up with that dumb switch?"

"I was about to ask you almost the same thing!" Carole snapped back.

"No way!" Stevie said. "I might, repeat *might* switch your boots, though I didn't, of course. But there's no way I'd put oats in my own. It's going to take me days to get all this dust and stuff out of them!" She stood up and carried both of her boots over to the grain bin and emptied them.

Carole and Lisa knew that the dusty remnants of the grain would be in Stevie's boots for a long time and that she would never have done that to herself.

"All right, all right, I'm sorry," Carole apologized. "I know you wouldn't have done that. You might be tempted to pull a silly trick like boot switching on your friends, but you'd never do a mean one on yourself!"

"You know, I never thought of boot-switching," Stevie joked. "It's a kind of neat idea. I wonder . . ."

Lisa looked over at Carole. "Come on," she said. "Let's get her dressed and off to class before she comes up with some bizarre scheme that will get her thrown out of this place!"

Carole helped Stevie to wipe oat dust out of her boots. Lisa folded her own street clothes neatly and was about to put them in her tote bag when she saw there was a small package at the bottom of it. Lisa unwrapped the envelope and discovered six chocolate kisses and a note from her mother saying she hoped she had a wonderful riding class.

"What's that you've got?" Stevie asked when she noticed Lisa clutching the little bag from her mother.

"It's just some candy I brought for us for after class," Lisa said, stuffing the note into her pocket. She wanted to share the candy with her friends, but she didn't like the idea of them knowing how her mother still treated her like a baby.

"Yipes!" Carole said, glancing at the clock. "Eight minutes to class and we haven't even tacked up yet. Let's go!"

Eight minutes later, the three girls appeared at the entrance to the outdoor ring, breathing hard from all the effort it had taken to get the horses ready for class in such a short time. It was practically a miracle they'd made it at all.

"Mount up!" Max said. Carole and Lisa brushed the good-luck horseshoe and quickly mounted.

"Have you got a problem?" Max asked, seeing that Stevie hadn't mounted Comanche.

"Sort of," she said, hiding her head behind the horse's neck. Lisa had the feeling that Stevie was trying to hide something.

When Lisa looked carefully, she realized exactly what she was trying to hide. Stevie had been in such a hurry to get to class that she'd forgotten Comanche's bridle! He still had on his halter and a lead rope. The whole class looked over and saw her mistake at the same time. Everybody, including Max, burst into laughter. Stevie was laughing the hardest.

Maybe we're wrong. Maybe it is still the silly season. Lisa thought to herself.

5

"I'M GLAD TO to see you've finally begun turning your practical jokes on yourself," Veronica simpered to Stevie after class. "I really liked the no-bridle trick." Veronica was standing near The Saddle Club as they changed into their street clothes. Stevie glared at Veronica. Although it *had* been very funny at the time, the look on Veronica's face made it seem stupid and embarrassing.

Stevie turned to Carole and Lisa. "Some people," she said, "have all the personality of a fingernail scratching a blackboard."

Veronica spun on her heel and returned to her own locker.

37

"Way to go!" Carole said, patting Stevie on the back.

Stevie grinned impishly. "No, the way to go is to my house where my swimming pool awaits. You did bring your suits, didn't you?"

"Of course we did," Lisa said. "We might not have too many good days left—"

But she was interrupted as the locker area was invaded by a large group of young Scouts. They were the same girls they'd seen in the supermarket.

"It worked!" Stevie declared proudly, jumping up to stop two of the Scouts from dismantling a harness in the tack room. The rest of them flooded over to the box where the stable's latest litter of kittens was trying to get some sleep.

"Ooooooh, cuuuuuute!" the little girls cooed together.

"How'd your rice concoction come out the other day?" Lisa asked the girls.

"Oh, it got burned, it was gross and disgusting!" one of the kids told her.

Lisa suppressed a smile. She hoped the little girls would be more successful as riders than they were as cooks. If not, pity the poor horses!

"Time to go," Stevie announced, flinging the rest of her clothes into her backpack and heading for the door. Lisa took a final look at the little girls. Red O'Malley, the head stableboy, was trying to explain to them what tack was. The girls weren't listening at all. One of them started braiding some stirrup leathers together.

38

Lisa and Carole exchanged glances and fled after Stevie. There were plenty of times when they'd be willing to do extra chores at the stable, but the thought of spending another minute around the little brats was just too much.

"I CAN'T BELIEVE how well your crazy scheme is working," Carole remarked to Stevie. The three girls had changed into their suits and Carole was trying to make her beach towel lie flat on the lawn so she could stretch out on it. Every time she lifted it up, the breeze twisted it.

"And I can't believe Max is going to let those little monsters ride our poor horses!" Lisa moaned. "Could you believe that one *braiding* the stirrup leathers?"

"We were bratty little kids at one time, too," Stevie reminded her.

"Never like that," Carole said. "Max is going to have his hands full!"

"It'll be better than having them empty, which is exactly what will happen if he runs out of money and Mr. diAngelo takes over Pine Hollow!" Stevie reminded her friends.

"You know," Carole said. "We're trying to help Max, but I'm not sure it's working. When I was rinsing Diablo's bucket today, I heard Mrs. Reg tell Max that 'that man' called again. Max said he hoped she'd hung up on him. That's no way to treat a diAngelo!"

They nodded in solemn agreement.

Carole sighed, then turned and lay on her stomach,

soaking up the late summer sunshine. As usual, Stevie was talking nonstop. She chattered about how she could call other people and tell them about Pine Hollow, then suddenly switched to the subject of Veronica diAngelo.

"On a scale of one to ten, I hate her twelve and a half," Stevie said.

"Fifteen," Lisa said, without lifting her head from her towel.

"Yeah, fifteen," Stevie agreed. "Maybe more."

Carole listened, amused by her friends. She thought about Pine Hollow and how much it meant to her—to all of them. "You know what I'd really like to do," she said, interrupting the auction, which by then had advanced to twenty-five on the hate scale. "I'd like to find a way to show people all the really good things they can learn at riding classes."

"You mean a horse show?" Lisa asked, propping herself up on her elbows.

Carole turned over and sat up. "Maybe, I guess," she said. She tugged a piece of grass out of the lawn and began chewing on it methodically. "Sort of."

"But the stable already had a horse show this summer," Lisa reminded her.

"And our gymkhana!" Stevie added. "Don't forget that. Wasn't that good enough?"

"Oh, it was great, especially when we won," Carole said quickly. "But those things were more for people who already know about Pine Hollow. The only people in the audience were our families and other riders. No, I was thinking of, like, a demonstration for other people in the town so that they might decide to come ride at Pine Hollow."

Stevie swung around and sat up, too. "I think she's on to something," she said to Lisa. "Can you see it now? Our names in lights!"

"Actually, I was thinking more of posters," Carole said. "Like if we come up with a neat idea for a show of some kind, we can put posters all over town."

"And we can charge admission and get money for Pine Hollow that way," Stevie said.

Carole shook her head thoughtfully. "We can't charge admission," she said. "The whole idea would be to make people want to come for fun—not because they have to pay."

"Well, they'll have to pay to take lessons," Stevie thought aloud. "And they'll want to once they see our demonstration."

"Of course we'll do something," Lisa said. "It'll be so neat."

"Yeah, but what? That's the question," Stevie said.

"How about a drill team performance?" Carole said.

"Do you think we could do something worth watching?" Lisa asked dubiously.

"Why not?" Carole answered. Then she turned to Stevie. "You never did get to ask Max about starting the team up again, did you?"

Stevie shook her head. "I got too upset about that phone call, but we can all go together before our next class."

"I really liked those practices," Lisa said. "Even when we all ended up practically bumping into each other. But it was fun—and with a little bit of imagination, you could see how good it could be."

"*Could* be if we practiced like crazy," Carole added.

"Well, why not?" Stevie asked. "We're crazy, aren't we? Horse crazy, anyway, right?"

"We're going to have to practice a lot," Carole continued. "Drill routines are awful if they're not done right. At least three times a week until . . . When are we going to do this?" she asked Stevie.

"Two weeks?"

"Never mind horse crazy, you're just *plain* crazy," Carole announced. "Lisa, I think we should throw her into the water until her head clears."

Lisa's eyes lit up. "Great idea," she said.

The two of them stood up and grabbing Stevie's hands, began pulling her over to the pool. Stevie laughed a lot and didn't put up much of a fight, but just before her friends began to push her into the water, she jumped, yanking them into the pool with her. The three of them made a tremendous splash, landing in the waist-deep water. Carole and Lisa were so surprised that they couldn't help shrieking when they hit the water.

Stevie took a big breath and ducked under the surface.

Carole and Lisa were standing in the water giggling when Stevie jumped up out at them, splashing wildly.

The three girls spread out in the water and began splashing each other. Lisa discovered that if she stood in one place and spun around, running her hand on the surface of the water, she could douse both her friends at almost the same time. They discovered the same thing. Soon it was almost impossible to tell who was splashing whom, but it felt wonderful.

After a few minutes, the activity subsided. All three girls lay back in the water and floated contentedly, gazing up at the blue sky, brushed white here and there by some clouds.

Carole turned over and lifted her head out of the water. She looked closely at Stevie. "Has any of this cleared your foggy brain?" she asked.

Stevie nodded. "You're right," she said. "Two weeks is out of the question. How about three?"

Carole was about to pounce on her and dunk her when Alex, Stevie's twin brother, yelled from the house.

"Lisa, phone for you! It's your mother!"

Of course it's Mother, Lisa thought to herself. She pulled herself out of the pool with a sigh, wrapped herself in her beach towel, and proceeded into the kitchen, dripping as little water as she could manage.

Five minutes later, she stomped back to the pool. Lisa, normally cheerful and optimistic, looked very angry.

"What's the matter?" Carole asked.

"Bad news?" Stevie asked.

"My mother is the bad news," Lisa said, grimacing. "I don't know what's gotten into her. She was phoning from down the block, just to ask me if I had put on any sunscreen. Can you believe it? I'm thirteen years old and I don't need to be told what to do every second."

"Maybe she's just showing she cares," Carole said.

Lisa regarded her carefully. Carole's own mother had died when she was younger and Lisa didn't want to hurt her friend's feelings. Lisa hadn't met Carole until after Mrs. Hanson's death, but she was pretty sure Carole's mother would never have pulled a stunt like that.

"Maybe," Lisa said. "But enough is enough!" Lisa was a little surprised to hear herself saying that. For years, she'd always done exactly what her mother wanted her to do. That was why she started riding in the first place. Now that she'd discovered riding and The Saddle Club, she didn't want her mother to interfere. "There's caring and there's being a bother—which rhymes with mother. . . ." she mused. "Sort of, anyway."

"Four weeks?" Stevie said, interrupting Lisa's thoughts. "Think we could be ready then?"

"Maybe," Carole said. "It's a possibility, anyway. Let's see."

Lisa used her towel to dry her hair and then sat down again and began putting sunscreen on her arms.

"Think Max will let us do it?" she asked.

"We won't tell him," Stevie said. "He'll be so surprised!"

"Shocked might be a better word," Carole said. "We're going to have to tell him sometime. And, after all, he's going to know that we're practicing and he's going to have to help us, isn't he?"

"We can worry about that later," Stevie said, dismissing the problem lightly. "For now, let's see what we can remember about the drills we were working on. First, there was the cloverleaf. . . ."

6

LISA SMOOTHED HER clean white blouse and adjusted her riding jacket. She stood outside Max's office with Stevie and Carole. The three of them had arrived early, done their chores, and dressed quickly so they could have a few minutes to ask Max about drill classes before their regular class began. Lisa ran her fingers through her soft brown hair. She wanted to impress Max, though she knew that the only way to impress him was to ride well. She glanced at Stevie and Carole. Carole looked just fine. She always did. Stevie, on the other hand, looked a little bit messy. There was a smear of dirt on her jeans. Her shirt hadn't seen an iron in several washings, and her boots were dusty. In short, she looked just like Stevie. Lisa smiled to herself, knowing Max wouldn't care about that at all.

The door to Max's office opened. A woman who looked vaguely familiar stepped out. She smiled at the girls as if to say hello and then walked toward the door to the stable.

Stevie peered into Max's office.

"Can we see you?" she asked.

"What about?" Max asked, sounding slightly irritated. The phone rang. Max answered it and while the girls waited, he scheduled a new rider for a first lesson.

Max looked at Stevie expectantly as he hung up the phone. There was no time to waste. Max was obviously busy and Lisa knew they'd better not make him late. Lisa nudged Stevie.

"We want to start our drill team again," Stevie began. When Max looked interested, Stevie went on. "We got so busy with the gymkhana before that we just couldn't work on it, but we liked it and we want to do it some more. Can we have drill team practice? Please?"

"Yes and no," Max said after a moment's consideration, but before he could explain himself, the phone rang again. He picked it up. It was another hopeful new student. Lisa noticed that Stevie was smiling when she saw Max write down the name. It must have been one of the people she'd called.

Max looked up at them again after he'd finished talking on the phone. "I'm glad you want to get back to drill work again. It's fun and it's excellent practice. If you had asked me this a week ago, I'd have jumped at the opportunity to teach you. However, just in the last few days, I have been absolutely flooded with new students. I can't turn these people away, I'm sure you understand. . . ."

Do we ever! Stevie thought.

"Anyway . . . I'd like you to be able to do drill work. Could we make a deal? Could you check with Mrs. Reg and see if there's a time when you could use the ring to practice by yourselves and if and when I have a few minutes free I'll come give you some tips?" He looked at the girls apologetically. "I have a good book here," he said. "I know it's not the same thing as an instructor, but if you read it carefully . . ." He turned around and took a volume from his full bookshelf and handed it to Stevie. "I think you should start by reading the section on beginning drills. The man who wrote the book was a student—" The phone rang again. Max answered it. He listened for a while and the girls waited patiently.

As they watched, though, Lisa noticed that Max's face was getting red as it did when he was angry about something. His eyes got steely. She had the awful feeling he was about to explode. But he didn't. He stayed calm. Too calm.

"I've already told you," he said, coldly. "It's an issue of money and time and I don't have enough of the first and you won't allow me enough of the second. The answer is *no!*" He hung up and looked up at the girls. Lisa thought he seemed surprised to see them still standing there. That meant it was time to go.

"Thanks, Max," she said, speaking for The Saddle Club. "We'll see you in class."

"Yeah, thanks for the book," Stevie said.

The girls glanced at one another and left Max's office quickly.

"See what I mean?" Stevie said when they reached the tack room. Lisa saw. So did Carole. It sure sounded like Max was in trouble. Lisa was very glad that they were already at work to help him out.

CAROLE TOOK A velvet-covered hard hat from the wall where they hung. All the riders were required to wear them at all times when they were working with the horses and riding. She checked the size and put it on. Her friends did the same.

Then, they turned to retrieve the proper tack for their horses. Each horse had tack that had been specially selected and adjusted to it. It meant that when the rider tacked up the horse, she didn't have to adjust every single strap—just the ones needed to put on and remove the tack. In the tack room, there were saddle racks and bridle brackets with each horse's name above the equipment, arranged in the same order in which the horses were stalled.

As soon as Carole took the bridle off Diablo's bracket, she knew something was wrong. Diablo was a spirited horse who needed a bit that would get his attention. Diablo would have a picnic with this bit!

"I think those little Scouts messed up the tack!" Carole said furiously.

"They sure did!" Stevie responded. "Look at this pony-sized saddle on Comanche's saddle rack. It would look like a postage stamp on my horse!"

"There's no way Max can let those brats ride here if this is what they do when they just come to visit the place!" Carole said indignantly.

"Wait a minute, wait a minute," Lisa interrupted the tirade and tried to calm her friends. "Something may be a little messed up, but it can't have been those girls. In the first place, Red was with them and he wouldn't have let them mess up. In the second place, the girls were here two days ago. There have been other classes in between. So, it's just a little confusion. Somebody made a mistake." Lisa turned to pick up her own tack. "And that somebody also messed up Pepper's tack. Look at this!" Suddenly all reason fled and she was furious. Lisa held up a Western bridle. It was definitely *not* the right bridle for Pepper. "Give me a break!" she said, now as angry as her two friends.

"And only ten minutes until class," Stevie groaned.

Carole looked around. "There has to be an answer," she declared. "We just have to figure out what it is." She began examining the other tack racks. Although their classmates had already taken their tack, it appeared, from the remaining tack for the horses that wouldn't be used in their classes, that the tack for the other horses hadn't been switched around. That meant that somebody had deliberately mixed up the tack on *their* three horses. This was somebody's idea of a joke.

"Some joke," Carole said, disgustedly.

"About as funny as mixing up our boots," Lisa said.

. "That was easy to solve," Carole reminded her as she began sorting through the extra bridles.

"You wouldn't say that if you still had oat dust in your boots," Stevie said.

The girls nodded. Somebody had a pretty strange sense of humor and was pulling some mean tricks on them. She wondered if the other kids in the class were having the same kind of jokes pulled on them. She thought she would have heard about it, but since The Saddle Club spent most of their time with one another, they might not always know.

"Here! I think this is Diablo's bridle," she said, locating it in the middle of a large collection of spare bridles. "And this one next to it could be Pepper's. Do you recognize it?" she said, holding the bridle up for Lisa's inspection.

Lisa looked carefully. One bridle looked pretty much like another to new riders, but Lisa was becoming an experienced rider and she could tell the difference.

"I think that's it," she said. "It looks like it, anyway." She took it from Carole's hand. Then she saw the nick in the leather of the reins that she'd felt so often and had come to use as a guide for correcting the length of the reins. "Definitely," she said. "Thanks, Carole."

"You're welcome," Carole told her, replacing the incorrect tack on the racks. "Now let's solve Stevie's problem."

"Stevie's problem is easy," Stevie said. "I just went to the pony's tack rack and found the biggest saddle there. It's Comanche's. I've made the swap and now we've got exactly six minutes until class. We'll never make it on time and Max is going to be really teed off. He cares so much about promptness, you practically have to have a doctor's note to be five minutes late."

WHEN THE GIRLS arrived at the ring four minutes after the start, Max just glared at them. There was no point in trying to tell Max about the mix-up with the tack. It wasn't the sort of thing he'd be sympathetic to. Promptness was very important in Max's book. Excuses weren't.

Embarrassed, they joined in on the exercise. Max was having the class do a sitting trot without using stirrups. For Carole, this was easy. She'd been doing it for a long time. But for the less experienced riders, it was very hard because it required good balance, and good balance was hard at a bouncing gaitlike trot.

She took the opportunity to look around at her classmates. She watched Veronica, especially. Much as she disliked Veronica, she had to give her some credit for

being a better-than-average rider. She wasn't having any
trouble with the exercise either. In fact, she was smiling
smugly as her horse circled the ring.

Then a thought occurred to Carole and she didn't like
it at all. *Why is Veronica smiling smugly?* Was it because
she was well-balanced on her horse? Maybe. Was it because she had just played a mean trick on some of her
classmates by switching tack on them and thereby getting them into trouble. More likely, Carole thought. *But
why?* After all, Max would get really angry if he learned
about it. *But there would be no way he could punish Veronica
if her father took over the stable!* Carole shivered at the
thought.

No, she told herself. *That can't be the case. Veronica is
looking smug because Veronica always looks smug.*

She hoped she was right.

LATER THAT DAY, Lisa slunk through the back door of her mother's car and slid down on the seat, hoping no one could see her. The problem was that her mother had come to pick her up after class and when she'd explained that The Saddle Club was having a drill practice, her mother had insisted on *watching* so she could wait to drive her back home again.

"That was so interesting, dear!" Mrs. Atwood said.

Interesting wasn't the word. The practice had been a disaster. The girls had forgotten everything they'd known about drill work and spent entirely too much time arguing with one another and with their horses. Drill work

54

was supposed to be precision riding, like military marching formations or halftime bands at football games. Their practice had looked more like the antics of the Three Stooges!

Aunt Maude, seated next to her mother in the front, nodded. "Oh, yes! And how did you get the horses to all come together at the center at the same time?"

"They weren't supposed to do that, Aunt Maude," Lisa said with more patience than she felt. "The horses are supposed to pass in front of and behind one another where the circles cross in the center of the ring. . . ."

"Oh, but I liked it the way you did it, dear," Aunt Maude said reassuringly.

"And did you like it when Stevie's horse shied, and mine started bucking?"

"You stayed on so well! I'm sure the judges would like that," Aunt Maude said.

Lisa sighed. "You get points for staying on a bucking horse at rodeos, Auntie," she said. "In English riding, you lose points for letting the horse buck in the first place."

"Oh, dear," her aunt said. "Then what about the sort of roping thing when one of your friends chased down the other girl's horse for her? She'd get points for *that*, wouldn't she?" she asked.

Aunt Maude was referring to the lowest point of the practice. Stevie had dismounted from Comanche to pace off her circle, hoping she'd be able to control Comanche's timing better. Uncharacteristically, Stevie had gotten careless and dropped Comanche's reins. The poor horse had had about enough of the hopeless practice by then, too, and had walked off toward his stall. Carole had had to intervene. At that point, Comanche had decided to play tag and began running freely around the ring. He'd even come close to jumping the fence, but Carole and Diablo caught up with him just in time.

"Wouldn't that be worth a lot of points?" Aunt Maude asked insistently.

"I guess so," Lisa said. It was easier to agree than to explain. She looked out the window of the car, wishing she were walking with her friends instead of driving with her mother.

"As soon as we get home, dear, I want you to change your clothes. You and I are going with Aunt Maude to the decorator store at the mall this afternoon. I want to choose a new wallpaper for your room. What do you think of a turquoise? We can then recover your chair in matching fabric. I'd like a white flounce on your bed and a solid bedspread—or would you like it to match the wallpaper and the chair? How about a sort of English country chintz?"

What was the *matter* with her mother?

"We just redecorated my room last year, Mom," Lisa reminded her. "I don't want to do that again. I like it the way it is."

"You do?" Mrs. Atwood said, sounding hurt.

She had an annoying way of making her feel guilty, but Lisa didn't like to hurt her mother's feelings. It was time to be tactful. "Yes," she told her mother. "You did such a nice job of it last time that it doesn't need to be done now."

That closed the subject temporarily, but unfortunately, it wasn't the only subject on her mother's mind. "I heard about a wonderful woman in town who gives computer lessons," Mrs. Atwood said a few seconds later. "They're being given at the Club," she began.

"Mother, I take computer at school," Lisa reminded her. "And besides, I've already taken ballet, piano, and painting, plus horseback riding. That's enough."

The car pulled into their driveway. Lisa got out of the back seat and escaped to her room before her mother could suggest that they sit and have a "nice little snack" in the kitchen. Lunch was going to be ready in a little while. Lisa didn't want to spoil her appetite.

Lisa showered and put on clean clothes. She retreated to her room, and took her book off her beside table. It was a book on riding.

A moment later she heard a knock. "Lisa dear!" her mother called. "Open up, please. I have something for you."

Lisa opened her door. In spite of the fact that she hadn't wanted a snack, her mother had brought her milk and cookies. Homemade cookies. She smiled polite thanks at her mother, took the snack, and retreated to her bed with a sigh.

Lisa had a passion for organization and logic. Some of the things going on around her didn't seem very logical, and it upset her. She went over to her desk and took out a pen and some paper. She wanted to make a list of the possible reasons for her mother to be behaving so strangely.

"1. Hates horses," she wrote. Her mother thought girls should know something about riding, just like they should know something about tennis, golf, sewing, and cooking, but that didn't include being horse crazy. Since Lisa had spent so much time at Pine Hollow, her mother was definitely cooling on the subject of horses.

"2. Something to do with Aunt Maude." That had real possibilities. Her mother was often overbearingly concerned with her, but it seemed to have stepped up since Aunt Maude's arrival. It was quite possible this didn't have to do with her so much as it did with another family issue, Lisa thought. Then the word "family" echoed in her mind and she had a weird thought.

"3. Misses my brother?" Lisa wrote. Lisa's brother was away at camp for the summer. Was it possible that she was simply upset about that? It seemed unlikely as an explanation for the overbearing motherliness. Besides, she'd never showered so much attention on Lisa's brother. He wouldn't put up with it. Lisa had always just accepted it. Only now, there was too much to take. She was acting like a total mother hen.

Mother . . .

Her pen nearly shook as she wrote her next thought—a possible explanation for weird behavior:

"4. Pregnant?"

Could that be possible? Lisa was almost 14 years old! *No way!* she told herself, hoping that wasn't just wishful thinking. But pregnant women got strange cravings for food, not interior decorations, she reasoned. Not computer lessons! Homemade chocolate chip cookies, maybe? She shuddered at the thought.

Lisa looked back over her short list and reconsidered each possibility. Number four was too weird. Number two was too vague. Number one made *some* sense.

Except at dinner that night, Mrs. Atwood kept talking about how interesting the drill practice was. And then, for dessert, she served red gelatin with bananas in it, from a horse-shaped mold!

Does red gelatin with bananas in it qualify as a strange food craving under number four? Lisa asked herself. What can it mean if it's shaped like a horse?

FOR THE NEXT couple of weeks, things seemed fairly normal. Lisa's mother continued to be too much of a mother, but Lisa got used to it. The Saddle Club had classes three times a week, and drill practice three times a week, too. Max was too busy with all his new students to notice the frenzy of activity at the drill practices. But from time to time, as he passed by the ring where the girls were yelling at one another and trying to control their horses, he would note that there was steady improvement.

"Better!" he said one day—and from Max that was a big compliment. Then he followed up with, "Lisa, don't forget to keep your toes in. Stevie, stop talking to your horse in English. Comanche talks sign language. Tell him what you want him to know with your legs and your hands. Carole, sit back in the saddle!"

Lisa wondered, as she had from her very first lesson, how Max could see so many things wrong at the same time!

After practice that day, the girls were going to begin publicity work for their show. Lisa had made a flyer on her family's computer and it even had a picture of a horse on it. Stevie had her mother take it to her office to copy. Mrs. Lake's secretary had made them copies in blue, yellow, and red to put on local bulletin boards and in shop windows. They were going to paint some large posters too.

"Come on, let's pack it in for the day," Stevie said. "I don't think I can do that cloverleaf one more time!"

"I don't think we've actually done it once," Carole said pointedly.

Stevie looked like her feelings were hurt, but Lisa thought there was some truth to what Carole had said. She also thought Stevie had a point. "So, we're not perfect. We're not even *good* yet," she said to her friends. "But enough is enough. We've been at it for more than an hour and we're tired. The way we feel right now, we're not going to get any better. Stevie's right. Let's quit for the day. It's time to stick the posters up."

Carole paused for a moment, glancing at both of her friends. "You're right," she said. "You're both right. Let's go post posters. Where do we start?"

"We start right here," Lisa said sensibly. "Mrs. Reg sometimes sends out a newsletter to riders. Maybe she'd include some of our posters."

"Hey, great idea!" Stevie said as the girls dismounted and led their horses back to their stalls. "Let's finish up here and then give her some posters before we leave."

"What?" Mrs. Reg said as she looked at the small posters Stevie handed to her. "What is *this*?" She pointed to the posters in her hand.

"It's a little drill show we're going to put on," Stevie said, hoping to calm Mrs. Reg.

"You've scheduled a show here without telling me about it? Without *asking* me about it?"

"We didn't think you'd mind," Lisa said, adding her calming words to Stevie's.

"We thought you'd be excited for us," Carole said. "We've made *so* much progress with our drill work. . . ."

"All that yelling at one another I just heard," Mrs. Reg said. "That's progress?"

The girls nodded sheepishly.

"A lot of progress," Stevie said. "Anyway, we've scheduled the thing for a Friday afternoon at a time when there are no ring classes—only trail rides. It must be okay. Isn't it?"

Mrs. Reg frowned. Normally, Mrs. Reg was a cheerful, supportive person. A lot of the riders, including The Saddle Club, really liked her and almost thought of her as a mother. Now, however, her face was dark, her temper was short.

"Maybe, maybe," she snapped. "It might work, but it shouldn't happen this way. You should *ask* me before you plan something like this. You should probably ask me in writing. I should talk to Max to make sure the stableboys will be free. But you've already made all the plans. Without asking me." She looked at the poster carefully and then flipped through the pages of her plan book.

"There's a lot of strange stuff going on here these days," Mrs. Reg continued. "I never saw so many new students—and every single one of them needs to ask me a million questions. There's stuff getting all mixed up in the tack room and Max has been storming around here like he doesn't know what to do with these young riders. Did you hear the racket when those Scouts were here?" Stevie squirmed uncomfortably where she stood. Mrs. Reg didn't seem to expect an answer to her last question. Stevie was glad about that.

"And the locker room! A couple of times a week, there's another mess in there, and nobody to own up to it! What is this, some kind of spa where the staff spends all its time pampering the guests? It is not! It's a stable. It's a working stable and right now, nothing seems to be working. Now, I've even got to schedule some kind of spur-of-the-moment drill show!"

Grumbling to herself, she continued shuffling through her calendar. Her hands found the right place in her plan book and she began to write something in, glancing back and forth between the poster and her schedule.

"Here," she said, looking back up at the girls. "You're in the book. It's done. I'm sending out a mailing in a few days. I'll enclose these, too." She put some of the posters in her top drawer with the plan book and closed it shut, firmly.

Stevie grinned. "Oh, thanks, Mrs. Reg. I knew you'd do it!"

"Thanks very much," Lisa said.

Carole nodded her thanks to the woman, too. "I'm sorry if we caused you any trouble," she said.

"Hmph!" Mrs. Reg said, reaching for the catalog she'd been reading when the girls arrived. She looked at it intensely. The girls knew they'd been dismissed.

In unison, they spun around and returned to the locker room.

"Phew!" Stevie said. That said it for all of them.

WHILE STEVIE AND Carole finished packing their riding clothes into their backpacks, Lisa fetched their sodas from the refrigerator. Max and Mrs. Reg always kept soda there for the students. Since the Saddle Club girls had their drill work after class, their sodas were still waiting for them—sort of. Lisa found that on each of the three cans set aside for them, the top had been snapped and the sodas had gotten flat.

"At least it's cold," Lisa said, handing each girl a can of flat soda.

"Swell," Stevie said, taking a swig and then pouring

the rest of the can out in the sink. "I think I'll drink water instead."

"We could stop at TD's and get something there," Carole suggested.

"Sure," Stevie agreed. "We need to put notices up at the shopping center anyway. Okay for you?" she asked Lisa.

Lisa nodded. "It's okay," she said. Her mother and Aunt Maude were visiting the Smithsonian Institution twenty miles away in Washington, D.C. It was a *very* big museum. They'd be gone for hours.

LISA WASN'T SO lucky on the day of her next class. Her mother insisted on driving her over and on staying for both class and drill practice. Nobody else's mother was there. It might not have been so bad if Mrs. Atwood had just sat there. But Mrs. Atwood wasn't a silent sitter. Every time Lisa had passed where she sat, her mother had waved or applauded or smiled. Lisa wished she'd been invisible.

Stevie and Carole didn't like seeing their friend so uncomfortable, but there really wasn't anything they could do to help her. They tried their best between class and drill practice. Carole took Mrs. Atwood to the tack room and introduced her to Mrs. Reg. The girls hoped that the two women would get to talking and Mrs. Atwood would forget about drill practice. It didn't work. As soon as the three girls were back in the ring, Mrs. Atwood reappeared.

"Here I am, dear!" she said, waving brightly to Lisa. Lisa sighed.

It was all Lisa could do to concentrate while her mother watched. Carole was trying to teach her how to get Pepper to change his lead while he was cantering. The horse's different gaits always followed a definite pattern of footfalls, distinct to the gait, but in cantering, it could start on either the left or the right side. When a horse changed leads in a canter, it had the effect of making it look as if the horse were skipping and it looked really elegant. Carole wanted them to incorporate it in their drill routine. Lisa was having trouble getting Pepper to follow her signals—or perhaps more correctly, she was having trouble giving Pepper signals to follow!

Finally, after an hour of near total frustration, Pepper came to a grinding halt and refused to move.

"I know exactly how he feels," Lisa said. "I don't want to move either."

"I guess that makes it time to stop," Stevie said sensibly.

Carole nodded agreement. "You've almost got it," she said. "You'll get it next time. Pepper will, too, you'll see. We'd have to stop anyway—I've got an orthodontist appointment."

"And I promised my mother I'd clean the pool," Stevie said.

"Is it time for me to take you home, dear?" Mrs. Atwood asked from the sidelines. Lisa glanced over at her.

In spite of herself, she smiled. Her mother always seemed to be there whenever she thought Lisa might need her. Of course, that wasn't necessarily when Lisa *actually* needed her. At that moment, what Lisa needed more than anything was some time away from her mother. She had to think fast.

"I can't go home yet, Mom," she said.

"I know. You have to change, don't you?"

"Well, yes, but I have some chores to do," Lisa fibbed. She'd actually done all her chores as soon as she'd arrived, but there was always more work to do at Pine Hollow. She'd find something, and Mrs. Reg would no doubt be glad to have her help.

"I'll wait, darling," Mrs. Atwood assured her.

"No, Mom. It could take a long time. You go on home now."

"But how will you get home?" she asked.

Lisa thought quickly. This was a catch question. She smiled. "I'll call you when I'm done," she said. "You can come pick me up then, okay?"

"Okay," Mrs. Atwood agreed, rising slowly from the uncomfortable wooden bench. "I'll hear from you later, then. Good-bye, Stevie and Carole. Can I give either of you a lift?" she offered.

"Oh, no thanks," they said in a single voice, almost too fast.

After Mrs. Atwood left, the girls took their horses back to their stalls, removed their tack, resupplied their hay, and gave them a little bit of water. The girls worked efficiently and, for once, didn't talk much among themselves. Lisa knew that both of her friends were feeling a little sorry for her because of the strange way her mother was acting these days. She didn't much want to talk about it and they could sense that. When they finished with the horses, they changed back into their street clothes. Stevie and Carole left to go their own ways, leaving Lisa to the quiet solitude of Pine Hollow in the late afternoon.

She took a saddle down off its rack, grabbed the can of saddle soap and a small bucket of water, and began to work at removing the grimy build-up.

As she worked, one of the stable's cats emerged from behind a feed-grain box where it had been hiding, probably trying to corner a mouse. Pine Hollow, like most stables, kept cats around, and they were expected to work for their living. This was a grey tiger kitten—a product of the most recent litter. His name was Justin Morgan. All of the cats at Pine Hollow were named after famous horses. This kitten—stocky, but strong and determined—had been named after the founding horse of the Morgan breed. It seemed appropriate.

Justin watched the stirrup leathers that dangled to the floor while Lisa worked on cleaning and polishing the saddle. The kitten remained in a crouched position, watching every twitching move of the leather. His body stayed immobile. His eyes followed the action, and his ears twitched. He was waiting for exactly the right moment.

"You've sure got patience," Lisa remarked to the kitten. "I wish I could have it like you do. I need your kind of patience with my mother."

"What did you say, Lisa?" Mrs. Reg asked from her office, which adjoined the tack room.

"I was just talking to Justin," she said. "He's planning his attack on some stirrup leathers."

"If he's interested in stirrup leathers, chances are he didn't get that mouse I heard him chasing," Mrs. Reg said. She walked into the tack room and stood near Justin, putting her hands on her hips. "Get to work, now," she said. "You know what your job is, don't you?"

The kitten glanced up at her quickly, and Lisa hauled the stirrup leathers up off the floor and began soaping them. When the kitten looked back and saw that his target had disappeared, he stood up and slunk off, back behind the grain box, presumably to find his mouse again.

"Good," Mrs. Reg said. "Now everybody's working." She smiled at Lisa. "But what are you still doing here? I thought your mother was going to drive you home."

"She wanted to," Lisa explained. "But I thought I ought to put in some time on these saddles."

"Hmmm," Mrs. Reg said. Lisa thought that meant that Mrs. Reg knew Lisa wasn't telling the whole truth.

"Don't work too hard," Mrs. Reg said.

"Why not?" Lisa asked. It wasn't like Mrs. Reg at all to suggest that riders shouldn't work too hard.

"I remember a horse we had here once," Mrs. Reg said, settling down on the bench next to Lisa. She took the bridle that was paired with the saddle Lisa was working on and began cleaning it with another sponge. "Name was Camille."

Lisa cleaned and polished silently. Mrs. Reg had a way of knowing an interesting story about a horse or a rider that would fit every situation. She couldn't be hurried when she was telling her stories, though. Lisa had learned early on at Pine Hollow to be quiet when Mrs. Reg was in a storytelling mood.

"Her owner got this idea that she was frail. And for a while, old Max was fooled into thinking so, too." Old Max was Mrs. Reg's husband, and the father of Max, Lisa's teacher. The students sometimes laughed that the Regnery family ran out of names after they discovered "Max." "Anyway, Camille surprised us. At first, she was healthy and robust, but as time went on, she got weaker and weaker and harder to ride. Max had the vet look at her whenever he came by, but he couldn't see anything wrong with the horse. After a while, as the horse kind of broke down, the woman who owned her was so upset that she hardly ever came to the stable. Then the horse started to get better."

Lisa furrowed her brows trying to figure this one out. There was, she had learned, always a reason for the stories that Mrs. Reg told. She waited patiently as the tale unfolded.

"So, when the horse became healthy again and her owner returned to ride her, Max watched over them very carefully. It turned out to be very simple. The problem was that the woman was crazy about her horse and always tried to do everything for her. She always showed up with an apple or a lump of sugar or carrots or some leftover from her own table. As you know, it's not a good idea to give horses too many treats, because they come to expect them and can be ill-mannered if they don't get them. But even worse, this woman was giving Camille so many treats that she was losing her appetite for foods that were really good for her. The poor horse was suffering from an overload of love!" Mrs. Reg soaped the cheek strap carefully, keeping Lisa thinking.

"Too much of a good thing?" Lisa suggested.

"What?" Mrs. Reg said, as if she hadn't heard Lisa because she'd been concentrating too much on the cheek strap.

"What happened?" Lisa asked.

"The horse was fine," Mrs. Reg answered. "Had a foal the next year. Max bred her to one of our stallions."

"No, I mean, what happened to the owner?" she asked.

"Oh, she was just fine, too," Mrs. Reg said. "As soon as the foal was born, she *really* had her hands full."

Mrs. Reg finished soaping the bridle. Lisa couldn't believe how fast she could clean a bridle. "There," Mrs. Reg said, satisfied with her work. She hung the bridle back up on the bracket and retreated to her office.

Lisa was almost done with the saddle. She finished cleaning the last expanse of leather and looked at the gentle sheen of the dark brown saddle. She thought about Mrs. Reg's story about the horse, Camille. What was Mrs. Reg trying to tell her.

Foal? Camille had a *foal*? Lisa's heart jumped into her mouth.

"Oh, no!" she said out loud to nobody.

CAROLE PUSHED THE "start" button on the stereo and mounted Diablo. Her friends were waiting on the other side of the riding ring for the music to begin.

"One-two-three, and . . . she said as the marching band began blasting out "The Stars and Stripes Forever." On the second count of four, the horses began moving where their riders wanted them to go. The girls were working on an exercise that had proved very difficult in the past. Starting from the edge of the ring at equal distance from the others, each rider was to make her horse trot in spirals, like the groove of a record, so that the three would meet in the center. It took a lot of precision because if the girls didn't watch out, the horses got all bunched up together while they were still supposed to be apart.

The music helped the girls to establish an even pace, but it didn't solve everything.

"Slow down, Stevie!" Carole warned.

"*I* slowed down already," Stevie shot back. "It's Comanche who keeps trying to catch up to Pepper!"

"Very funny," Carole returned. "Try using a little pressure from your outside hand to slow him down."

"Maybe you guys should just go faster," Stevie suggested. But just then Comanche responded to Stevie's signal and shortened his stride.

"Good!" Carole said excitedly, for she could see that if all three of them maintained their pace exactly as it was, they'd succeed, meeting precisely in the middle of the ring.

"Very good!" Max's voice boomed over the music. He had paused on his way across the ring to watch a few minutes of their practice.

A small part of Carole wanted to smile. A larger part made her face a picture of determination and concentration. She didn't want compliments from Max to distract her. She only had eyes for her friends. She watched them as carefully as they watched her, and each other, until the magical moment when they were at the center of the ring. Their horses were still trotting, now nearly head to tail, in a tight circle.

"Now slow to a walk," Carole said. The horses changed gaits at the same instant. She allowed herself to smile then. "And stop," she said quietly. The music came to a climactic end. The horses stood still. The three girls grinned.

"We did it!" Stevie yelled, patting Comanche enthusiastically on the neck. "We really, really did it."

"We really are getting better," Lisa said, almost in disbelief

"Yeah, maybe we *will* be good enough by next Friday," Stevie said.

"What's happening Friday?" Max asked. He pushed the "off" button on the stereo and joined the girls in the center of the ring.

The girls glanced nervously at one another. One thing they *hadn't* planned for was how to tell Max about their surprise.

"What's happening next Friday?" he repeated. There was a little sharpness in his voice.

Lisa and Stevie looked to Carole. She knew they would. Lisa might be the oldest of them, and Stevie might be the boldest, but when it came to handling Max, they expected her to take the reins.

Carole didn't have the faintest idea what to say. She leaned forward in the saddle and patted Diablo. "Well," she began. "It's sort of a surprise."

"I don't like surprises," Max said. "Especially when they have to do with my stables, my riders, and my horses."

"You'll like *this* one," Carole told him reassuringly. "We've been working for weeks and weeks on our drills and we think we've gotten good enough to do a demonstration. So, we've invited a few people to come watch us work next Friday at six o'clock. You can come, too."

Max's face darkened. "I can't," he said. "And you can't either."

The girls stared at him in disbelief. They had thought about all the different kinds of reactions he might have to their plan, but refusing to let them do it was not one of them.

"Why not?" Stevie asked. "What's wrong with it?"

"You didn't ask my permission, for one thing," he said. "For another, there's something else going on here then."

"But people are planning to come," Carole protested. "We've sent out announcements already and put them up all around town!"

"Then you're just going to have to take them down," Max told her, his face now stormy.

"But—" Stevie began.

"No buts," he said. Before they could try again, he turned and left them.

"How could—how can . . ." Lisa spluttered at his retreating back.

"All that *work!*" Stevie groaned. "And it's for his own good!"

"But he doesn't know that, does he?" Carole reasoned.

It was not much consolation.

LISA FELT EMPTY inside as she walked home. Stevie and Carole each had things they had to finish up at the stable, so she walked by herself. She could have used a friend right then, though it didn't seem likely that either of her fellow club members would have been able to think of anything to be cheerful about.

After she'd untacked Pepper, and while he was cooling down, she'd knocked on the door to Max's office to ask him to reconsider. "The answer is still no," he'd said without even looking up. Lisa found out that Carole and Stevie had each tried, too, with no more success.

On one hand, Lisa could see that even without putting on a show, she and her friends had learned an awful lot just practicing. Drill work required a special kind of riding and tremendous concentration. Their purpose, however, hadn't been to do something for themselves. They'd wanted to do something for the stable—and especially Max. But it wasn't going to work.

She kicked at the gravel angrily and only succeeded in filling her sneaker with gritty dust. Disgusted, she sat down by the side of the road and untied her shoe. As she worked to get the dirt out of it, she thought about the whole mess. No matter how she looked at it, it didn't get any better. Sullenly, she stood up and continued on her way home.

Her outlook didn't improve when she arrived at her house. Her mother was busily baking yet another batch of something in the kitchen. Lisa passed right through, ignoring her mother's cheerful greeting and the promise of a "delightful" surprise awaiting her. Lisa was determined to retreat to the comforting solace of her room.

She slammed the door behind her and tossed the backpack onto her bed. She tugged her still-gritty sneakers off, threw them in the general direction of her closet and flopped down on her chair.

But it wasn't her chair. It didn't have the comfortable, familiar feel of the nice soft overstuffed chair that had occupied the window corner of her room for several years. She stood up to stare at the thing. This chair was a super-modern contraption. All chrome and foam. It wasn't the kind of chair you could curl up in to read a book or sprawl across to study history. It wasn't a chair that Lisa liked at all.

"Mom!" she yelled.

Her mother came running and appeared breathlessly at her door. "Isn't it wonderful?" Mrs. Atwood said excitedly, her face glowing with excitement while she pointed to the despised chair. "I looked and looked until I found just the thing for you." Mrs. Atwood smiled proudly. "It's the latest in design. Melanie Antwerp told me about this fabulous store at the mall. I knew you'd love it—" Then, for the first time, she noticed the look on Lisa's face. "You *do* love it, don't you?" she asked.

Thoughts flashed through Lisa's head. The thing about Lisa's mother was that she cared—a lot. Lisa knew her mother really had spent a lot of time looking for the horrible chair *and* that she'd genuinely thought Lisa would love it. This was the "delicious" surprise her mother had promised when she'd walked in the kitchen door. She had put so much thought and time into a project that didn't need doing—and wasn't that the story of Lisa's mother's life these days? She was forever fixing things that weren't broken. Just looking at her mother's face, Lisa knew that it would break her heart if she told her how she actually felt about the situation. There had to be a way. . . .

"What did you do with my old chair, Mom?" she asked calmly.

"I put it in the den for now. I'll have to recover it because it doesn't match at all, but we can do that later."

The den, Lisa thought. That gave her an idea.

Lisa told her mother how much she appreciated her spending all the time, and money, on the beautiful new chair. Lisa admired the design and styling of the thing. "But," she said. "Wouldn't this actually look better in the den than in here?"

Mrs. Atwood looked at her thoughtfully. "I suppose," she agreed. "But I want you to have the new chair if you want it. . . ."

"Oh, no," Lisa protested. "The whole family should *share* the new chair."

"Hmmmm," Mrs. Atwood said. Before she could object, Lisa told her mother that she'd ask her dad to help her switch the chairs after supper.

"Okay," Mrs. Atwood agreed. She sounded a little bit as if her feelings were hurt, but Lisa knew they weren't hurt nearly as much as they would have been if Lisa had told her what she'd *truly* thought about the new chair.

Her mother returned to the kitchen, where a timer bell was ringing insistently. Lisa sat back down in the uncomfortable chair and tried to think. She couldn't think in it. She took a shower instead. She could always think in the shower.

Later, when it was almost dinnertime, Lisa decided to take her mother-troubles to a higher court: her father. She thought of it when she looked out of her window and saw him struggling with the outdoor grill. She skipped downstairs and hurried out the back door.

"Would you like to help me shuck the corn?" her mother suggested as she flew by.

"No, I'm going to help Dad," she said. The screen door slammed behind her.

"With the *grill?*" her mother asked. Mrs. Atwood never touched their grill. Lisa knew that her mother felt barbecuing was a man's job. Lisa wasn't so sure that her father felt the same way.

"Here, Dad, let me help," Lisa offered. He was about to remove the dusty used charcoal.

"Don't get dirty, honey," he said.

She shrugged. "I don't mind. Besides, I need you to help me with something in return."

He looked at her quizzically. Lisa put the lid of the grill

on the ground, removed the grate, and began sifting through the debris for reusable charcoal. Her father held the plastic bag where she deposited the dusty ashes.

"It's about Mom," she said, scooping a small shovelful into the trash bag. A cloud of gray ashes rose out of the top of the bag. "Looks like a volcano, doesn't it?" she asked. "The ashes, I mean, not Mom."

Her father nodded, patiently holding the bag. Lisa continued.

"It's like she can't leave me alone," Lisa explained. "She has this idea of things she ought to be doing, and that I ought to be doing—"

"And that *I* ought to be doing," her father said, nodding towards the barbecue grill. "She's always been that way," Mr. Atwood reminded her.

"But it's getting *worse*," Lisa said. She took the cleaned-out grill and set it straight up again.

Out of the corner of her eye, she could see that her mother was fretting while she watched Lisa work with her father. Her mother probably didn't want Lisa to get dirty. Lisa thought she was a little old for her mother to spend time worrying about things like that. She told her father so. He agreed.

"I tried to figure out what's going on, Dad," Lisa said. She swallowed uncomfortably. She didn't want to ask the next question, but her father waited while she collected her thoughts—and her courage. "Dad," she began. "Is Mom pregnant?"

Her father smiled and then chuckled.

"Is she?" Lisa asked, bolder now.

"No, hon. She isn't. I was just laughing because I remember when she was pregnant with you. She just sort of put her feet up for the whole time. It was just the opposite of this flurry of activity."

He poured fresh charcoal into the grill and put the electric starter onto the coals. Lisa readjusted it so that it was touching as many of the coals as possible. "Works better that way," she explained.

"Thanks," he said. "You're better at this than I am. You should do the outdoor cooking."

"Mom would *die*," she said.

He nodded in agreement. "Listen, Lisa," her father said, putting his arm around her shoulder. "I know Mom's being sort of a nuisance these days and I'm not sure what it's all about myself. I do know that she loves you, and me, and I have the feeling this will all work out. For now, have patience. I don't know why I'm saying that to you. You've got loads of patience. I have an idea. But sometimes you have to be careful what you wish for; it might just come true!"

10

THAT NIGHT, STEVIE studied the bottles of nail polish in front of her. Carole and Lisa were at her house for an after-dinner Saddle Club meeting. Stevie had decided that they could polish their nails while they talked about horses.

"Carole, you try the sparkly pink. I'm going to use the deep red. Lisa, you get green."

"Green? Why *me?*"

"It'll be good for you," Stevie told her. "You always want to do what people expect you to do. So, do something different. After all, it's the silly season, isn't it?"

Without further comment, Lisa reached for the green

nail polish and unscrewed the top. She took out the little brush and began painting her nails a deep forest green. She finished one nail.

"I don't know if it's still the silly season," she said, admiring her green pinkie nail. "I think it may be the mystery season. Not only is my mother up to her same weird stuff, but my father's getting mysterious, too—"

"Pickles and ice cream?" Stevie asked. "Dad always teases Mom about the strange stuff she ate, especially when she was pregnant with Alex and me. Maybe that's why I'm so weird!"

Lisa and Carole smiled at their friend.

"No, Dad promised me she's not pregnant," Lisa said. "He's noticed her doing weird things, too, but he didnt 't tell me what was causing the situation, or what he was going to do to solve it. Just said he had an idea. Wouldn't say what."

"Speaking of not saying *what*," Carole said. "What is going on with Max?"

"Now that *was* weird," Lisa said. "Maybe some sort of mysterious disease is sweeping the adult population these days." Lisa had finished one hand. She held it out so her friends could admire her work. "Now, I think I'll do the other hand in bright red. Then I can cover my face with my hands and hide in a Christmas tree!"

Stevie grinned, and then turned to Carole. "See, it's working," she said.

Carole began giggling. "You really think you can keep

Lisa from being logical and normal just by having her polish her nails?"

"In the silly season, anything can happen!" Stevie declared, reaching for the green nail polish herself.

"CAROLE, LISA, AND Stevie, please report to the office. Carole, Lisa, and Stevie!"

Carole cocked her head in curiosity. She and her friends were in the middle of their afternoon chores before their drill practice, though Carole didn't know why they were bothering with drill practice after Max's edict the other day.

What on earth could be so important that Max would have then interrupt *chores*? She took one more shovelful of wood chips and spread them on top of the peat in Diablo's stall. He watched her silently, but responded with an affectionate nicker when she patted him on his silky neck.

"Don't know what this is about, boy," she whispered into his ear, "but I hope Max isn't still angry with us."

The horse nuzzled her neck and tickled her. Carole stowed the shovel in the equipment closet and headed for Max's office.

She met up with Lisa and Stevie at the door to Max's office. Lisa had her hands shoved into her pants pocket. Carole glanced at her.

"I didn't have time to take off the red and green polish," she explained. "I don't want Max to think I'm crazy."

Standing between them, Stevie put a green-polished hand on Lisa's shoulder and a red-polished one on Carole's. "He already knows I am," she joked.

They went in.

"Stop and go?" Max asked, looking at Stevie. He had noticed her nails first thing.

Stevie and Carole relaxed a bit. If Max was joking, then he wasn't angry any more. But Lisa blushed and shoved her hands further into her pocket.

"Listen," he said. "Mrs. Reg told me that you girls told her about the show and she okayed it. So, it turns out that the problem is really that I should have told her about *my* plan, but it was supposed to be a surprise. She assumed you'd already told me about yours. I assumed she knew about what I was doing. She couldn't tell you because she didn't know what it was that I hadn't told her and the whole problem comes down to the fact that I've been busy out of my mind with one billion new students here which is great but it's awful, too. You know what I mean?"

The girls exchanged glances. Carole wondered briefly if Max was losing his mind. She'd never heard him say anything so garbled.

"Are you okay, Max?" she asked, genuinely concerned.

"Oh, sure," he said. "I've just been too busy to pay attention to things I ought to be paying attention to," he explained. "And it's gotten me in trouble."

86

Trouble was where they had begun, and trouble seemed to be where they still were. There had been too many secrets for too long. Stevie, never very good at keeping secrets anyway, couldn't hold it any more.

"That's what we trying to help with!" Stevie blurted out. "You should be able to spend your time teaching and running the stable and not worrying about Mr. di-Angelo!"

"What's *he* got to do with this?" Max asked.

Carole poked Stevie in the ribs. Stevie clapped her green-nailed hand over her own mouth.

"Nothing," Carole said. And then to switch subjects as quickly as possible, she asked, "What was it you didn't tell Mrs. Reg that you should have told her?"

"Huh? Oh, that," he said. "Well, that's what I want to talk to you about. I thought it should be a surprise, but I'm beginning to get the feeling that surprises aren't always a good idea."

He paused. Carole had the distinct feeling that that was as much of a lecture as they were going to get. It was enough, though. They all certainly got his point.

"You remember me talking about my student, Dorothy DeSoto?" he continued.

Of course, they all knew who Dorothy DeSoto was. She was one of Max's most famous students. She'd gotten her start at Pine Hollow and had gone on to be a very successful and famous rider. She'd even been on the last Olympic team and had gotten a silver medal.

"Is she coming for a visit?" Lisa asked, awestruck.

"Better than that," Max said. "She's coming to do a demonstration for all of my students, especially you three. I've been planning this with her for weeks and it's scheduled for exactly the same time as you girls want to do your drill show. Dorothy is a very busy woman and I can't ask her to change her schedule—"

"But Max, we put all those signs all around town. Lots of people are going to show up for it. . . ."

"Most of them relatives," Max suggested.

Of course, that was true. The girls hadn't liked to think about it, but the chances of luring a lot of total strangers to an amateur drill show by three young riders were actually pretty slim.

"And those who do come will have the *extra* treat of watching Dorothy DeSoto do a dressage demonstration."

"Extra?" Carole asked suspiciously.

Max smiled slyly. "Sure, why not? We've both planned something for the same time. We can do both. Dorothy's demo will take about fifteen minutes. We'll put the two together and really give the audience a treat."

"You mean we're going to be on the same bill as Dorothy DeSoto?" Stevie said, obviously stunned. Carole thought it was very theatrical of Stevie to refer to it as "being on the same bill," but then, Stevie was a very theatrical person.

"Yes, that's what I mean," Max said. "Six o'clock on Friday. Don't be late. Don't make any mistakes. You'll go

88

first." Max stopped abruptly and looked at Lisa in surprise. She was so excited about the idea of performing for an Olympic rider that without thinking about it, she'd pulled her hands out of her pockets and was holding them against her cheeks.

"Go and stop?" Max asked. At first, Lisa didn't know what he was saying. Then she realized that she'd revealed her silly fingernails. Blushing deeply, and unable to answer, she shoved her hands back into her pockets.

"It's part of the drill exercise," Carole explained. "Has to do with left and right."

Max nodded. The answer seemed to satisfy him. "Anything to make things simpler," he said. "Now I just wish somebody could make *my* life simpler."

"That's what we were trying to do," Stevie said. Knowing that Stevie was reverting to her earlier topic, Carole glared at her. It sometimes seemed that Stevie's worst enemy was her mouth.

"How's that?" Max asked.

"I mean, putting both demonstrations on the same bill," Stevie stammered.

One of Max's eyebrows went down; the other went up. The look on his face was of total skepticism. "That doesn't make sense," Max announced. "Why don't you tell me what you really meant?"

Stevie scrunched up her face. She'd blown it and she knew it. "We were just trying to help," she began.

"With what?" Max asked.

Their goose was cooked. Stevie glanced at Carole for help.

"It was your idea. You'd better tell him," Carole said.

"Yeah," Stevie agreed unenthusiastically. "Max, we wanted it to be a secret, but we've just been trying to help you out so that you could pay off Veronica's father, see, because we hate the idea that he'd take over Pine Hollow and Veronica would be even more awful then—"

"Veronica's father?" Max said. "What's he got to do with this and besides that, how *could* Veronica be . . ." His voice trailed off. Carole had the feeling he didn't want to finish the sentence. "Anyway, for the third time, what does Mr. diAngelo have to do with this?" Max started to get a very serious look on his face—maybe even stormy. Carole was getting a bad feeling about the situation.

It was time to let the cat completely out of the bag. "Well, I heard you talking to him. You said you couldn't do it now, and you knew the riders would suffer. Well, we *would* if the bank took over this place. We just couldn't let it happen, Max!" Stevie waited. "You told him you didn't have enough money and you needed more time."

Max studied Stevie carefully. "When was this?" he asked.

Stevie thought for a second. "It was right after the class when we were playing Break and Out," she told him. "You remember—the one where Veronica was cantering and you'd told us all to walk?" Stevie smiled a little, remembering how silly Veronica had looked and how they'd all laughed at her. "Then after class I came to your office to ask you something and I heard you on the phone. You sounded just desperate! You said you didn't have enough money or enough time, and I, I mean we, figured it would be bad for all of us if you were in trouble, so we . . ."

She stopped talking. The girls could see that Max wasn't listening. He was thinking. He began to nod.

"I remember the conversation," he said. "And now I don't know whether to laugh or yell."

"Laugh," Stevie said. "Please!"

Max's shoulders started shaking and the girls knew that meant he was beginning to laugh.

"All right," he said. "I'll laugh. You thought I was talk-ing to Mr. diAngelo?" He snorted with laughter.

"Yes, I did," Stevie said indignantly. Although she liked it better when Max laughed than when he yelled, she didn't much like it when he was laughing at her. "You told him that you couldn't pay it now and that it was going to affect us, but we'd get used to it."

"Now let me guess—then you went out and began dragging in students from off the streets to keep me in business?" he asked.

The Saddle Club girls nodded in unison.

"Like those little Scouts, and that waitress, and all the fourth graders in Willow Creek?" he asked.

"The Scouts were just luck," Stevie said. "We ran into them in the supermarket."

"Whose luck?" Max asked. "You should try *teaching* them!"

Carole had a sudden and vivid memory of the girls wandering all over the supermarket, wreaking havoc. She tried to imagine what it must be like instructing a group like that. She burst into laughter. Lisa and Stevie joined her.

"Well, they're learning," Max said. "But they're exhausting. And so are all the other students you brought in here for me."

"But you're not going to have to sell out to Mr. diAngelo now, are you?" Stevie asked.

"No, and I never was," Max said.

"*What?*" Stevie yelped. She glanced at Carole and Lisa, who were shaking their heads at her. "Uh-oh . . ." she mumbled.

"What you overheard wasn't a conversation with him," Max continued. "I was talking to a man who was trying to sell me a horse. I want to buy a couple of new horses. I'd like some trained show horses for the better riders to use, but I've got so many boarders at this time that I don't have space. I told the man that. He was trying to push me into expanding, but I can't do it now. It's the busiest time of the year—especially since I've had so many new students. So I lost the chance to buy the horse he wanted me to buy. He was a terrible nag and kept calling me. I didn't like him at all. I'm glad our deal fell through."

"You mean you weren't talking about losing the stable?" Stevie asked, her face beginning to flush.

"No, I wasn't. This place has been in my family for three generations and it's not about to change hands. I guess I'm glad you care so much about it—"

"But we've caused you more problems than we've solved, huh?" Carole asked.

"Oh, I don't know," Max said. "You have caused me some trouble, but it's always good for a place to have new students. If only I had enough assistants to help me instruct them all—say, I've got an idea!"

"Uh-oh," Stevie said. "I don't like it when he gets that look in his face. It always means more work for us."

"It sure does," Max agreed. "I'd like you to assist me with the classes for some of the new students."

"You mean like help you teach?" Carole asked eagerly. To her, that sounded like a dream come true. It didn't sound like work at all.

"Yes," Max said. "Especially with those little Scouts!" Carole reconsidered. That *would* be work.

"Max, we're going to be awfully busy working on the show," she said quickly.

"Of course you are," he said. "Then right after that, you can begin helping me with the little girls. The first thing they have to learn is *not* to call me Maxie!"

"I think we can handle that!" Stevie said. Then they all laughed together.

As the girls left Max's office, Carole had a great feeling of relief. She hadn't liked keeping a secret from Max.

"Boy, I blew that, didn't I?" Stevie asked. She sounded disgusted with herself.

"Don't worry," Carole consoled her. "It's all going to work out okay. We'll do our show. We'll get to meet Dorothy DeSoto. The stable's not going to belong to Mr. diAngelo—"

"And we'll get to help Max teach the little monsters," Lisa finished for her.

"Hmmm," Stevie said. "I wonder."

"What?" Carole asked.

"Well, I think I'm getting an idea," she said thoughtfully.

"No," Lisa told her. "No more ideas!"

"Ever?" Stevie asked. She sounded just a little bit hurt.

"Well, at least for a week," Lisa relented.

"It's a deal," Stevie agreed. "Now let's go practice our routine."

They returned to the stalls.

"I think I'm going to die," Carole said as she carried the tack to her waiting horse. She put the saddle on Diablo and adjusted the girth. "Imagine—Dorothy DeSoto here! And she'll see us ride, too!"

Carole wasn't certain whether she was more scared or more excited. She was certainly both, and so were Lisa and Stevie.

"We can do it, you know!" Carole said, throwing her arms around her friends' shoulders. "We'll be great!"

She just wished she felt as sure as she sounded.

WHEN CAROLE GOT to Diablo's stall before The Saddle Club's next drill practice, she could tell that something was wrong. Diablo looked so tired. She slid the door open to get a better look at him. He stood listlessly in his stall, the white foamy sweat collecting on his shoulders and breast. He had the look of a horse who had been ridden hard. He was even still breathing fast.

"What's going on here?" Carole demanded. Nobody answered her.

Then Red O'Malley came along to Diablo's stall carrying a bucket with some fresh water for the horse.

"Who's been riding Diablo?" she asked. Red just gave

her a disgusted look. That could only mean one thing: Veronica had been riding him. She was the only girl at the stable who would expect Red to do her work for her, untacking her horse and bringing him fresh water. She was also one of the few riders who would have bad enough judgment to put him in his stall when he was still hot and breathing hard.

"*I* was supposed to ride Diablo this afternoon," she said.

Red shrugged. "Tell it to the judge," he said. "Or better still, the banker's daughter."

Carole nodded in resignation. "Okay, okay. I'll ride Barq. But I've got to have Diablo on Friday, okay?"

"Check with Mrs. Reg," Red suggested. "She can manage it, I'm pretty sure."

"All right," Carole agreed. She was about to go get Barq's tack when she stopped and turned back. "Does Veronica always put her horse away without cooling him down?" she asked.

"Veronica always does exactly what Veronica wants to do," Red answered.

Carole nodded in understanding. Veronica would never think of her horse before herself. "I'll walk him a bit," she offered. Diablo really needed to walk around the ring a few times before he got to drink and rest in his stall. Carole knew that if a horse didn't have a chance to walk and cool down, his muscles could stiffen up and he'd be in real trouble the next time somebody tried to ride him. Veronica knew that, too. She just didn't care.

"Don't worry," Red assured her. "I know Stevie and Lisa are going to be waiting for you, so go ahead and take Barq out. I'll walk Diablo, but thanks."

"You're welcome," Carole said. She returned to the tack room to pick up Barq's tack. As she went, she realized again how relieved she was to know that the trouble Max was in didn't have anything to do with Veronica or her father. That girl was enough of a pain as it was. But that *did* leave Carole wondering why Veronica had taken Diablo out for a ride. She *knew* Carole was signed up for Diablo. Could she have ridden him just to make Carole angry? Was that Veronica's idea of a joke? For that matter, could it be that Veronica's idea of a joke included things like switching boots, putting oats in them, and mixing up tack? Carole decided to think about it after drill practice.

STEVIE SNUGGLED UP to Comanche before she put on his bridle. She scratched him under his chin. As before, his mouth opened and closed as if he were chewing with his mouth open—or as if he were talking.

"How about it, big boy?" she asked the horse. "Ready for the stage?"

She then dropped her voice, began his jaw working, and spoke for him. "The one going west?" he asked.

"Cute," she said. "I just love a joker."

She began to tack-up the horse, thinking all the while about what a silly idea it was that horses could talk, and

97

whether she could use the idea. It had very real possibilities. She just needed to have a word with Max.

"NOW TO THE right—and then curve at the . . . Lisa!" Carole called sharply. "You've got to make those corners sharper."

Lisa sighed. It seemed to her like this was a day when she couldn't do anything right. "How do I make them sharper?" she asked sarcastically. "Break the horse in half to make a ninety degree turn?"

Carole looked a little surprised, then seemed to realize that she wasn't really being fair. "I'm sorry," she said. "I'll show you."

Carole began walking Barq. At the corner, Barq began not so much to turn as to bend. His entire body made a crescent and then turned back into a straight line when he'd completed the turn.

"Oh," Lisa said, almost involuntarily. "How'd you do *that*?"

"I'll tell you my secret," Carole said. Carole seemed to be most comfortable and happy when she was talking about horses and riding. Sometimes, Lisa thought, it got a little boring, but the fact was that Carole loved horses so much and she knew so much about them that she was usually right, and always worth listening to.

The girls worked together on turns for about fifteen minutes. Carole explained how the rider had to coordinate what each hand and leg did in order to tell the horse exactly what to do.

"Give me a break," Lisa said. "The horse can't possibly remember all those things!"

"That's right," Carole said. "He can't remember it all. That's why *you* have to remind him. Every time. Now try it."

Lisa was less than certain it was going to work. At her first corner, Pepper was very happy to do exactly what he wanted to—cut the corner improperly.

"See?" Lisa said.

"Try again," Carole told her.

Lisa regarded Carole dubiously, but she headed Pepper toward the next corner. This time, she tried to follow Carole's instructions. She sat deep in the saddle, looked straight toward the turn, shifted her outside foot back of the horse's girth and used her inside hand to indicate the turn to her horse. Like magic, Pepper's entire body curved with the turn. Lisa could hardly believe it.

"See?" Carole asked.

Lisa nodded sheepishly. "Let me try it a couple more times," she said.

Carole and Stevie watched and encouraged Lisa while she worked on the maneuver.

"You know one of the things I really love about riding?" Lisa asked. Her friends looked at her expectantly. "I love the fact that when you learn to do something right, you can really, actually control the horse. I mean, like it *works*."

Carole and Stevie both nodded and smiled. They knew *exactly* how Lisa felt. They felt the same way.

• • •

THE STABLE WAS quiet. Stevie was alone in the tack room, applying saddle soap to Comanche's tack. Stevie didn't usually go out of her way to spend time alone or to spend time cleaning tack, but her mother had left strict instructions with the housekeeper today that Stevie was to work on her book report the moment she got home from riding. If there was a surefire way to make a book dull, it was having to write a book report about it. Just sitting there, Stevie groaned at the thought. Anyway, as long as she was doing her chores at the stable, she *wasn't* writing a book report and that was good.

The tack room was between the locker area and Mrs. Reg's office. Mrs. Reg had gone to buy supplies. None of the students was around. Stevie's only company was a gray tabby cat named Hambletonian. The cat wasn't much company. He slept soundly in a beam of late afternoon sunlight which streamed through the dingy window. Every few minutes, his sunbeam would shift. Hambletonian would half open his eyes, notice where the warming beam had gone to, and shift his position. Stevie thought he must have eaten a very big mouse to be so lazy this afternoon.

Stevie soaped the skirt of the saddle. While she worked, she was going over the intricate movements of their drill exercise. She was concentrating so hard, and working so quietly while she did it, that she hardly noticed when somebody entered the locker area.

But the long shadows of the late afternoon played across the floor of the locker area and into the tack room. Stevie looked up, suddenly alert. Somebody was moving around the locker area and making no noise at all. There was something peculiar about that.

Staying quiet herself, Stevie looked through the door into the locker area. Somebody was crouched in front of Stevie's cubby and that somebody didn't belong there.

Silently, Stevie stood up and sneaked over to the door. She took cover behind a pillar where the shadows made a hiding place. She peered around the pillar and watched.

Veronica diAngelo was rummaging around in Stevie's cubby, in Lisa's, and in Carole's. Veronica removed the boots that each girl stored in her cubby. She took a bottle of something out of her pocket, opened it, smeared the contents on the soles of the three pairs of boots, and lined the boots up on the floor. Veronica glanced around to be certain nobody was watching—Stevie ducked back into the shadows for a second—then she sealed the little bottle, tucked it into her pocket, and tiptoed back out of the locker area, heading for the stalls.

As soon as Stevie was sure Veronica was gone, she hurried over to their cubbies to see what Veronica had been up to. All she could see was that the three pairs of boots had been taken from the Saddle Club lockers and lined up neatly on the floor. Stevie reached to pick up her boots and suddenly everything was clear as a bell. Veronica had put glue on their boots. They'd be stuck to the wooden floor!

Stevie tugged at all three pairs. It took quite a bit of force, but since she'd gotten there so soon after Veronica had left, the glue wasn't completely set. Very carefully, she laid each boot on its side. She sprinkled some wood chips on the part of the floor where some of the glue remained. The little bits of glue on the bottom of each boot would dry harmlessly and wear off quickly when the girls walked around in them.

That settled the matter of the boots and floor. But what about Veronica diAngelo?

Stevie returned to the tack room, quickly finished cleaning Comanche's saddle, returned it to its rack, and headed home. She had some phone calls to make!

12

"YOU'RE WEARING A patch in the rug," Colonel Hanson told his daughter. "And if you're practicing marching, I could suggest a group that would welcome you. Want to start with a twenty-mile run on Saturday at six-thirty?"

"Oh, Daddy!" Carole said. "I'm not ready for the Marines!"

"You sure look like you are," the colonel told her. "I can always tell—when your feet get working that hard, something's on your mind. Was it the phone call from Stevie?"

She had just gotten off the phone with Stevie, who had told her about the boots and the glue. She didn't know what The Saddle Club could do to counteract Veronica's idea of a practical joke. She flopped down in the chair facing her father. "Maybe you can help," she said.

"Maybe I can," he said.

"It's about Veronica diAngelo," she began.

"Maybe I *can't*," the colonel said.

"Well it can't hurt for me to tell you about it," Carole said.

"Okay," he agreed and then, as always, listened carefully. Carole told him about Veronica's tricks. And when she told him about the latest one with the glue and the boots, the colonel completely astonished Carole by laughing.

"Reminds me of something we did to our drill instructor," he said, still chuckling about the memory. "He never *did* find out who did it. . . ."

Carole regarded her father carefully while he continued laughing to himself. "Did you ever tell me this story?" she asked.

"Don't think so," he said. "But I think it's time you heard it."

She leaned forward in her chair and listened very carefully.

"WHAT WAS THAT call, dear?" Mrs. Atwood asked Lisa as she hung up the phone.

"It was Stevie," she said returning to her job of setting the dinner table.

"Is something wrong?" her mother asked solicitously.

"Hmmmm, not really," Lisa told her. "Actually, something is sort of wrong, but I think we now have a chance to solve it. In fact, a lot of things seem to be solving themselves these days."

"I know what you mean!" her mother said enthusiastically. "So why don't you put candles on the table?"

Candles? Candles were for special occasions, celebrations, birthdays. What was her mother celebrating? She certainly wouldn't be celebrating Stevie's phone call. But if her mother wanted to celebrate, that was okay. Lisa realized that she'd forgotten to tell her parents about the show on Friday, and so the candles would make it a sort of festive announcement. She opened the breakfront and removed the antique silver candelabra that had been a special wedding present to her parents. There were used candles in it when she took it off the shelf. If this were somebody's birthday, Lisa would have put new candles in it, but just to tell about a drill demonstration, Lisa thought the half-used candles would do. She placed the candelabra carefully in the center of the dining room table.

Lisa stood back to admire her work. She straightened out her father's napkin. Her mother's water glass was on the wrong side. Lisa switched that. She carefully centered the salt and pepper in front of her own place. She checked again. It looked perfect.

"Okay, come see," she invited her mother. Mrs. Atwood emerged from the kitchen and studied her daughter's work.

"Nice, very nice," she said. "But *do* put new candles in the candelabra, won't you?"

Mrs. Atwood disappeared back into the kitchen to stir her sauce.

Something was definitely up.

"GLUE! SHE WAS putting glue on our boots! Can you believe it?"

Stevie was sitting at her own dinner table a few blocks away from Lisa's. She was surrounded by her three brothers and her parents. On her plate was a piece of meat which she had attacked furiously with her knife.

"Are we subtituting minute steak for Veronica diAngelo?" Chad teased her.

Stevie looked down at the mess. "Don't I wish!" she said. "Now I have to find a way to get even. Any suggestions?"

"Water bombs!" Michael, her little brother, piped up.

"Nah, Veronica would know who'd done it right away," Alex, Stevie's twin, said. "Try something else. How about itching powder in her boots?"

"Nah, put it in her breeches!" Chad, her fourteen-year-old brother, suggested.

"Great idea!" Stevie said. "But what's itching powder?"

"Beats me," Alex said.

"I dunno," Chad said. "I just read about it somewhere."

"You could cut her riding pants into shreds," Michael said.

"It would take too long. Someone would see us," Stevie told him.

"How about you just snub her?"

"Yeah, the old silent treatment!" Chad said. "That works every time."

"We've been giving this girl the old silent treatment for years. She's never noticed. That's her problem."

"Well there must be something. . . ." Alex said.

"Yeah, something," Michael echoed.

"Really mean . . ." Chad said, thinking out loud.

"*Really,*" said Stevie.

Nobody spoke for a few minutes while Stevie and her brothers worked on the problem, which they saw as a joint challenge.

"Isn't it nice to see our childen working on a project together with such enthusiasm?" Mr. Lake remarked sweetly.

"Yes, and such kindness," Mrs. Lake said.

Stevie looked up from her shredded meat and glanced at her parents surreptitiously. For a second, she thought she saw them smiling.

"You wouldn't be smiling if you'd had to buy me a new pair of boots," she reminded them.

"You're right," her father said. "There must be some way to get back at her!"

Then the kids began laughing with their parents.

"HERE'S TO THE future," Mr. Atwood said. He lifted his wineglass. Mrs. Atwood held hers up, as well. Lisa took her milk and tapped both of her parents' glasses.

"I'm glad you mentioned that," Lisa said, after she sipped some milk. "There's something about the future, I mean the near future, that I forgot to tell you. The Saddle Club is putting on a show at Pine Hollow. We're going to be doing a demonstration of all the drill things we've been working on. And, even better than that, Max's former student Dorothy DeSoto will be doing a demonstration for all of us, too. She's just fabulous! You know she's a world-class rider?"

"How exciting, dear," Mrs. Atwood said. Lisa didn't think she sounded very excited, though.

"Yes, it *is* exciting," Lisa said. "It's on Friday at six. Then we're going to have a sleepover at Carole's."

"I'm glad you're going to Carole's," Mrs. Atwood said, surprising Lisa. "I won't be able to pick you up to bring you home."

"Well, you wouldn't have to bring me home," Lisa said. "As long as you're at the show, that's what's important."

"I'm sorry, dear. I can't be there," Mrs. Atwood said.

"You *can't*! Why not?"

"Well, because I'm going to be working that afternoon."

"Huh?" was all Lisa could say, in total confusion.

"Yes, dear, *working*," her mother told her. A giant smile of pride crossed the woman's face. "I've got a job. And from now on, you and your father—and your brother when he gets home from camp—are just going to have to stop relying on me to do everything in the house. You are all going to pitch in from now on. Hear?"

"Yes, I hear," Lisa said meekly. "But what kind of job is it that you can't come to my show?"

"It wasn't my idea," Mrs. Atwood began. "It was Aunt Maude's. It was because of all that time we spent at the mall, especially when we were buying those riding pants for you—"

Lisa groaned to herself. Her mother had the most roundabout way of answering a question of anybody she'd ever known.

"You mean you're going to be selling riding pants?" she asked her mother.

"Oh, no dear. *Modeling* them! Well, riding pants or whatever is necessary at the mall. See, there's a local modeling agency that all the stores in the mall use. When one of the stores wants a model for whatever purpose, well, they just call the agency. At Maude's suggestion, I registered with the agency. My first job is, in fact, modeling clothes for working women Friday evening. I just can't be at your show, too."

"But we've worked so hard!"

"You certainly have, dear. Remember, I got to see some of the practices and now I'm really glad that I did. It's too bad I can't be there. But I can't. Frankly, I'm a little disappointed that you can't come to my first fashion show. But at least your father's promised to be there."

Lisa stared at her mother in disbelief. Was this really the woman who baked cookies nonstop, who insisted on driving her daughter to places she didn't need to be driven, who wanted to remodel rooms that looked just fine? And now that Lisa really wanted her to be there, she was going to be too busy?

Lisa was about to tell her mother just what she thought of this when her father joined in on the conversation.

"Isn't it wonderful, Lisa?" he began. At that moment, Lisa didn't think it was exactly wonderful, but she listened. "Your mother's been doing so much for us all these years—remember, hon, we were just talking about it the other day, weren't we?" he asked pointedly. Lisa recalled their talk by the barbecue grill. Was this the "idea" he had hinted at? Mr. Atwood continued, "—and now she gets to do something she's always wanted to do. Your mom's a beautiful woman. Not a lot of women her age can still wear their college clothes! The agency was thrilled when she walked in the door. We're going to have to make some sacrifices around here, but it seems like very little compared to the benefits of having your mother do something that will mean so much to her."

Lisa decided she'd have to do some thinking before she did any more talking. She just smiled and nodded and finished eating her supper quickly.

It seemed that, in fact, a lot of questions *were* being answered these days. For instance, now she knew why her mother had wanted to put new candles into the candelabra. But there were new questions, too, like how come her mother's work had to interfere with something as important as the drill demo? It just didn't seem fair. After all, Lisa thought, couldn't she have gotten a job the week after the show?

13

"WE COULD TRY gluing *her* boots to the floor," Stevie said. She pulled a stalk of green hay out of the ground and began chewing on it methodically.

She was sitting on the top of a knoll overlooking one of the stable's paddocks, where the foal, Samson, and his mother, Delilah, were taking in the morning sunshine. Lisa and Carole were sitting with her, cross-legged in a circle. It was supposed to be a Saddle Club meeting, except at that moment, each girl was concerned only with her own problem.

"Look, after we do the pinwheel, I think we should go back and do the cloverleaf again. Our demo just isn't long enough. It needs more—even if more means repetition. Don't you think?"

Carole held her riding crop in her right hand. Idly, she slapped it against her left hand while she stared off into the distance.

"I just can't believe my mother isn't going to be there. My mother has been shadowing me for months—and now that I want her, she won't be there! Can you *believe* it?"

Lisa put her elbow on her knee and rested her chin on the palm of her hand.

The words each girl had spoken hung in the air.

"Carole," Stevie said plaintively. "You're not listening! How are we going to get back at Veronica?!"

"Oh," Carole said, almost surprised. "That's easy. We can switch boots on her." Lisa and Stevie looked at Carole, confused. Carole shrugged and then continued. "Well, it was Dad's idea. They did something like this to their sergeant. See, Lisa, the jodhpur boots you were wearing last spring are exactly like Veronica's, aren't they?"

Lisa tried to picture the low brown leather boots and then realized that they were, in fact, the same style and brand as Veronica had been wearing.

"Well, you've outgown them. They're a size six. Veronica's are a seven. We'll just switch your old boots for her new ones. They look the same. She won't know what happened, but her feet will be killing her!"

"Wonderful!" Stevie said, grinning widely. "It's just perfect. She won't even suspect."

"Right, and I never even bothered to take those old ones home. They're still in the back of my cubby."

"I'll make the switch when Veronica's doing her chores," Stevie volunteered.

"You mean getting *Red* to do her chores," Carole corrected her.

"Isn't it funny? She spends more time getting somebody else to do her work than it would take her to do it herself," Lisa remarked. "Being lazy is really hard work!"

"And this time, Veronica's laziness is going to pay off—for us," Stevie said. There was a wicked gleam in her eye. She held her hand up. "High fifteen!" she declared. The girls slapped their hands together.

"One problem down, two to go," Carole said. "We've just got to add something to our demo to make it longer. We've been working *so* hard, but it's still only about five minutes long."

"Oh, I already solved that," Stevie said. "Comanche and I have worked out a surprise for you."

"What is it?" Carole asked. She was more than a little suspicious.

"You'll see," Stevie said mysteriously. The stalk of hay was clenched in her teeth. She grabbed it with the tips of her right fingers and thumb and tapped at it with her pinkie as if it were a cigar and she were flicking off the ash. The motion was strangely familiar to Carole.

When Stevie's eyebrows began bobbing up and down suggestively, Carole recognized her Groucho Marx imitation. "Am I going to like this?" she asked.

"You bet your life!" Stevie said. And that was all she would say.

"But—what about me?" Lisa asked. "You each solved one another's problems. Who's going to solve mine?"

"What's your problem?" Stevie asked her.

"My mother and father can't come this afternoon. My mother's gone and gotten a job as a model at the shopping mall. She's not going to be home at all any more! Probably ever!"

Stevie looked at Lisa carefully before she spoke. "Sounds to me like your mother's solved your problem for you. Weren't you just complaining that she was always hanging around and doing things that didn't need to be done?"

"Well, yeah," Lisa said. "But this one *needs* to be done. *Your* parents are going to be at the show, aren't they?"

"Mom, yes, Dad, no, and two out of three brothers, yes," Stevie said, checking off her family members on her fingers.

Lisa looked to Carole.

"Sure, Dad will be here—along with one of my old instructors from the stables on the base."

"See?" Lisa said. "I'm practically being abandoned!"

Stevie and Carole looked at one another. "You want to go first?" Carole asked Stevie.

"Lisa, I've got two working parents, too," Stevie began. "Sometimes they're around, sometimes I'm on my own. Sometimes it's good; sometimes it's a pain. But they are almost never in my hair the way your mother has been. She probably tagged around after you because she didn't have enough to do. It doesn't seem so wonderful now, but you'll get used to it. It'll be more good than bad and when you've got something really important—"

"Like our show today?" Lisa challenged.

"Yes, like our show today," Stevie repeated. "Then you'll learn that if you give both parents some warning, usually one can be there."

"But neither of them can be here today!" Lisa pouted.

"Because you didn't tell them in time, did you?" Carole said sensibly.

"Why do you always have to be right?" Lisa asked Carole, only half teasing.

"Because I'm your friend," Carole answered. "And besides that, here's the good news. My old instructor, Major Madison, is bringing a video camera. Your parents will get to see the show after all."

"It's not quite the same, is it?" Lisa asked Stevie.

"True, but it's better than nothing. Right?"

"Okay," Lisa conceded. "I guess the pluses will outweigh the minuses."

"Well, that settles it," Stevie said matter-of-factly. "Carole solved my problem, I solved hers, and we both solved Lisa's. Everything's solved—club meeting is over!"

"Not everything is solved," Carole reminded her friends. "We still have to do a great job in our drill demo, don't we?"

"With a team like this, how can we miss?" Lisa asked.

"Just what *are* you going to do?" Carole asked, turning to Stevie.

Stevie only smiled. Carole thought she could practically see feathers at the edges of Stevie's mouth. She knew she and Lisa were just going to have to wait.

CAROLE LOVED THE preparations for the show. She had been grooming Diablo until his coat shone like glass. His mane and tail were brushed smooth, all the tangles gone. She'd even polished his hooves. His saddle and bridle gleamed with the rich, deep sheen of fine leather. She and her friends were dressed in identical outfits: fawn-colored jodhpurs and shirts with double rows of brass buttons. They looked really sharp, and a little bit military, which fit in with the drill work they were doing. She felt a little chill of excitement as she led Diablo to the outdoor ring.

Only the indoor ring at the stable had spectator seats, so that's where the show was going to be. The girls had to do their warm-ups outside.

Carole brushed the good-luck horseshoe and then mounted Diablo. Lisa was already riding Pepper and practicing spirals.

"This is so easy when there's only me," Lisa said.

"It's all in pacing," Carole reminded her.

Stevie appeared with Comanche. Without ceremony, she touched the horseshoe and bounded up onto her horse.

"Did you see?" she asked excitedly. She pointed wildly toward the area of the stable that opened onto the outdoor ring.

Carole and Lisa brought their horses over to the entrance. They leaned forward and peered down the dim hallway.

It was hard to see, but it wasn't too hard to see Veronica diAngelo. She was just returning from her private lesson on the trail with Red. She'd dismounted from Barq and she was positively hobbling as she led her horse to his stall.

"She can barely walk!" Stevie giggled. "Your dad's a genius!"

"Yeah, he is," Carole acknowledged. "But I may be even more of a genius than he is. What size are your jodhpur boots, Stevie?" she asked.

"Oh, I've got these giant feet. Chad says my shoes are violin cases. I wear an eight and a half. Couldn't you just see—Hey, you *are* a genius. I'll make the switch after the show tonight. She'll be swimming in them on Monday!"

"Two minutes, girls!" Max called out to them.

Carole felt a knot form in her stomach and she thought she could almost hear her blood rushing through her veins. Two minutes to showtime. Two minutes would show the results of all their hard work. Two minutes to success—or humiliation?

"One minute!"

"Come on, Carole. You're the leader. You go first," Stevie said. "If you're not scared, we won't be."

Scared? Of course I'm scared, Carole thought. *But I can't show it. We can do this. We've been practicing for weeks. We've done everything we can to make it good and to make it interesting. And besides, whatever we forget, our horses will remember. After all, they've done it as much as we have.* Carole smiled to herself. *Maybe we should just let them do it by themselves!*

"Okay, line up!" Max ordered them.

"Yes, sir!" Carole said in her best Marine Corps daughter's voice. "Saddle Club, let's go give this audience a show!"

Lisa brought her horse right behind Carole's. Stevie followed close on her trail. They walked to the entrance of the indoor ring. The girls could see that there were about fifty people to watch them, though they were no doubt more interested in Dorothy DeSoto.

Mrs. Reg stood in front of the girls, waiting to give them their signal to enter the ring. The girls and Mrs. Reg listened carefully for their cue.

Max stood in the middle of the ring. He explained to the audience that three of his students had been working on a special demonstration, which they wanted to perform for Dorothy DeSoto. That sounded a lot better than explaining about Stevie's dumb mistake, the girls thought.

. "And now I'd like you to welcome Carole Hanson, Stephanie Lake, and Lisa Atwood—The Saddle Club Drill Team!"

"Hey! We've got a name!" Stevie exclaimed.

"And I like the sound of it," Carole added.

"I can see it in lights," Lisa joked.

They didn't have any more time to think about fame and glory, though. Just then, Mrs. Reg pushed the button on the sound system and the very familiar music of "The Stars and Stripes Forever" began. Mrs. Reg moved aside to let the girls pass. "Smile!" she said and then waved the girls into the ring.

14

LISA COULDN'T BELIEVE the feeling she had as she entered the ring. She had a great big smile on her face, just like Mrs. Reg had told her, but everything was a blank. She could barely remember who she was, much less where she was, and even less what she was supposed to do.

Carole, directly in front of her, headed off to the left as she reached the center of the ring. Then, as if on signal, everything came back to Lisa. She knew just what she was supposed to do. Now, she only hoped she could do it.

Their first exercise was the cloverleaf. Each girl fol-

121

lowed a three-circle pattern that made them cross in the center at practically the same time. The trick was to not have it be *exactly* the same time. That was a collision course.

The horses trotted, almost in time to the music. That was the idea. The music, which seemed to the audience like a pleasant accompaniment, actually was very important to the riders and the horses. Lisa finished her first circle. Carole crossed first, then Lisa, then Stevie. And they didn't even come near colliding.

The audience clapped. Lisa could hardly believe it. But just because they managed one circle didn't mean they could do all three that the exercise called for. Pepper was picking up speed. Lisa shortened her reins. Pepper shortened his stride, but it was too late. She was going to get to the intersection first. Lisa knew it would look silly if she reined her horse to a stop. Besides, Diablo seemed to be going slower. Lisa bit her lip in concentration, crossed her fingers that Carole would see what she was doing, and rode through the intersection. Carole winked at her. She'd done the right thing!

After the third circle, the girls took their positions for their next exercise. As the audience applauded, Lisa prayed that it would go well. It was spirals and it was very hard.

The Saddle Club Drill Team rode their horses to the edge of the ring, equally spaced from one another. They would circle the ring four times, making each circle smaller than the last. If they were very careful, the horses would stay the same distance from one another and the only time they would come close would be at the center of the ring.

Lisa crossed her fingers and rammed her hard hat down on her head. She was determined. If this exercise wasn't done perfectly, it just looked silly.

Carole nodded. The music started and the horses began their trot. The music was a waltz, played on a calliope. They were supposed to remind the audience of a merry-go-round. Up and down, up and down, Lisa posted with the smooth motion of Pepper's trot. She didn't want to be too obvious about looking around at her friends, but Carole was in her line of sight and Carole was posting at almost exactly the same tempo as she was. It was working!

While each circle got smaller, the horses miraculously remained the same distance apart from one another. Lisa knew that the audience was seeing something that looked like a simple exercise because they were doing it right. In fact, because of a horse's naturally competitive spirit—catch up with the one in front of you—it was about as hard an exercise as there could be.

Exactly as the music ended, the three horses were just about head to tail in their smallest circle in the center of the ring. All three girls were so proud of their job that they couldn't stop grinning.

Carole started to say something to Lisa and Stevie, but she couldn't be heard over the applause.

"Everything else is duck soup," Carole whispered when the clapping stopped. "Pinwheel time!"

Normally in a drill exercise, ranks of horses would form lines, the left half facing front, the right half facing to the rear, and move in a counterclockwise motion. The horses in the center would just about turn in place while the ones on the end would canter to keep up. With only three riders, that was impossible, but they'd adjusted the maneuver to suit their small numbers.

Carole was the pivot, Lisa was to be next to her, Stevie on the end. Somewhere along the line, though, Comanche and Pepper seemed to have picked a fight with one another. Comanche didn't want to let Pepper into the formation.

"Come on!" Carole hissed, urging Lisa to bring Pepper up next to Diablo, but Comanche was already by Diablo's side and didn't want to let Pepper in.

Comanche kicked.

Pepper snorted.

Carole groaned.

This was not Lisa's idea of duck soup.

"Comanche!" Stevie said. Lisa could see her gripping her horse tightly with her calves, trying to show Comanche who was in charge. Lisa tried the same thing with Pepper. Pepper turned around and gave her a look that seemed to tell her to mind her own business.

"This is my business," Lisa hissed at her horse and gripped tighter. Obediently, Pepper tried to move up in between Diablo and Comanche.

Comanche bucked.

Pepper darted backwards.

The unexpected motion made Lisa slip. She was near losing her balance and shifted her weight quickly. The audience went "Oh!"

Lisa righted heself. The audience sighed, "Ah."

Lisa looked over to Max, hoping he would give them some help. Max was watching carefully, but there was no sign at all that he was going to come to their aid. Lisa could feel herself getting angry at him. After all, they were *his* students. *He* should help them!

But Lisa knew that wasn't the way it worked at all. It was Max's job to teach them everything he could, and one of the things he'd taught his students was how to control their horses. He wasn't going to interefere with the way they were doing their jobs. He was going to let them succeed on their own. And they *would* succeed. After all, Max had taught them.

Lisa took her riding crop and touched Pepper gently on his flank. She almost never had to use a crop on Pepper, but now she did. A small reminder was all it took. He stepped forward with determination. Stevie had obviously come to the same conclusion. Lisa could see that she was putting pressure on Comanche's left side to move over and make room for Pepper. The horse balked briefly, and Stevie tapped *his* flank with the crop. He stepped aside. Before Comanche could change his mind, Lisa made Pepper scoot between the two horses. The audience applauded. Lisa didn't think they should have clapped then. The horses were just doing what they should have done in the first place.

Carole nodded. The music began again and the girls began their self-styled pinwheel.

Carole and Stevie each reached out a hand to Lisa, holding their reins in one hand. Lisa dropped both her reins, and held Carole's and Stevie's hands at shoulder height. When they signaled with their legs, the horses began moving. Diablo, the pivot horse in their pinwheel, turned in place. Pepper, next out on the pinwheel, moved slowly. Comanche, at the end of the pinwheel, had to move the farthest and the fastest. The girls only used their legs to guide their horses and they *never* had to let go of one another's hands.

The audience burst into applause and the girls felt giddy with joy. It worked—it really worked! When the music stopped, Lisa just couldn't help it. She held her hands up on either side of her and Stevie and Carole gave her high fives at the same moment.

Knowing the demonstration was over, Max stepped into the ring, clapping proudly for his students, and shook hands with each of them.

"Nice job, girls. Really nice! All your work showed. Congratulations."

Usually a gigantic compliment from Max was "Not bad." Lisa felt warm and happy all over. She could hardly wait until her parents saw the tape. They'd love it. She knew they would.

Carole and Diablo began to head for the stalls. There would be a little break and then Dorothy DeSoto would do her demo. Lisa sighed with relief and joy and followed Carole.

The two horses entered the stable area where the girls dismounted. Lisa patted Pepper hard to congratulate him and then hugged him around the neck. Carole was doing the same with Diablo.

"What a threesome!" Lisa declared.

"Yeah!" Carole said. "We were great. A trio that can't be—" She paused. "Speaking of trios, though, where's number three? What happened to Stevie?"

The two girls dashed back to the entrance to the ring just in time to watch Stevie's surprise.

Stevie was leaning forward as she sat on Comanche. Her face was on the right side of his neck, where the audience could see it. Her hand reached toward the horse's chin, out of sight of the audience.

"You were a naughty boy, Comanche," Stevie said loud enough to catch the attention of the audience in the ring. There was a smattering of laughter from the audience. Something was up and they knew it. They just didn't know what, yet.

Then, to everybody's astonishment, the horse began "speaking." Stevie turned her head so the audience couldn't see her mouth moving, just Comanche's. She dropped her voice and talked for her horse. "It was just a little horse play, Stevie," he said.

"Are you going to start that again?" she asked.

"Sure, why not?" the "horse" retorted.

"Because you're supposed to be crossing the ring and going back to your stall now," she told the horse.

"Speaking of that," he said, ignoring her suggestion, "do you know why the chicken crossed the road?"

"Yeah, to get to the other side," Stevie said.

"Nope," Comanche contradicted her. "To get a copy of *The New York Times.*"

"I don't get it," Stevie said.

"Neither do I," Comanche told her. "I get *The Washington Post!*"

The audience began giggling. From where Lisa and Carole stood, they could see that Stevie was making the horse "talk." The audience certainly knew he wasn't really talking by himself, but Stevie was doing such a good job of hiding it when she was talking for him that everybody almost believed it.

"Very funny," Stevie said.

"Say, Stevie, did you hear about the guy who dug three holes in his front yard?"

"No, I didn't," said Stevie.

"Well, well, well," the horse said.

Stevie winced. "Ooh, I walked right into that one, didn't I?"

"Splash," he agreed.

"You know, Comanche, these people here think that a horse and his rider are a perfect pair—"

"Then they've never been saddled with the likes of *you*," he retorted.

"Cute," she told him. "I bet you expect me to bridle at that sort of remark."

Lisa and Carole began giggling.

"I can't believe these awful jokes!" Lisa said.

"Stevie specializes in them," Carole said. "Hey, check out my dad! He and Stevie have the same weird sense of humor."

Lisa looked at the audience. There was Colonel Hanson, laughing so hard he was almost crying. "He's really loving it, Carole," she said.

"Yeah," Carole agreed.

"He's loving it about ten time more than my parents would be. You know, I think I'm glad they're not here. They wouldn't even get most of these jokes."

Carole put her arm around Lisa's shoulder. "Things have a way of working out sometimes, you know."

"I guess they do," Lisa said. "Thanks."

"Wanna bet?" Stevie was asking Comanche.

"Sure, I'll bet you twenty bucks."

"Not the kind of bucks you tried earlier," Stevie said warily.

The audience began laughing again. Comanche turned his head around to look at his rider. She just shrugged her shoulders.

Stevie dismounted and gave Comanche a hug. Then, trying not to grin while the audience clapped, she led him off into the stable area where her friends were waiting.

"You were wonderful!" Lisa exclaimed.

"And so was Comanche!" Carole joined in. "When did you think of doing that?"

"Oh, it was all his idea," Stevie said vaguely, pointing to her horse. "I just thought it would be fun."

"Well, it was. It was loads of fun," Carole said. "And you were terrific!"

"Nice job, girls," Max told them. He was standing next to the same woman they'd seen in his office the day they'd asked him if they could begin the drill team again. She was holding the reins of a horse they didn't recognize. It could only be Dorothy DeSoto!

"I really enjoyed it all—even the talking horse," Dorothy told The Saddle Club. "Max has certainly expanded his curriculum since I was one of his students!" she said, grinning.

"Actually, the girls did most of it themselves," Max said. "Except for the jokes. Comanche learned them all from me."

For a second, it looked as if Dorothy believed him. Then she burst into laughter.

"All right, girls, go put those horses in their stalls quickly. I don't want you to miss Dorothy's demonstration, so you can finish bedding them down after the show is all over."

"We'll hurry!" Carole promised.

"Don't worry," Dorothy said. "I'll wait for you."

The girls put their horses away and untacked them as quickly as they could. Within a few minutes, they were returning to the ring—this time as part of the audience. But there was no sneaking in. As soon as the audience saw them, they began applauding The Saddle Club Drill Team. Very pleased with themselves, the girls waved to their fans and then took seats to watch Dorothy's performance.

The music began. Dorothy had prepared a program that had her highly trained horse going through all the important movements of dressage. The horse followed nearly invisible commands. He seemed at one moment to be skipping, at another to be walking sideways. She got her horse to turn circles with his hind legs, leaving his front ones in place, and then to do the same thing in the reverse—moving his front legs in a circle around his hind legs. He trotted slowly. He trotted quickly. She got him to do a pace, which was like a trot, except that the horse's legs moved together on each side, so that both left legs went forward, then both right. On some horses, that was a natural gait. When it wasn't natural, it was *very* hard to teach. Then the horse cantered, first leading with one leg, then with the other. When he changed leads, it made him appear to be almost flying.

The whole thing was absolutely astonishing and beautiful. Although the demonstration lasted about ten minutes, it seemed to be over in a flash.

When the applause had died down and the audience stood up to leave, Stevie walked back to the stable area, led by her friends, almost in a trance. "Thirty-two separate exercises! Can you believe it? She's wonderful!"

"Yeah, but I never made a horse talk!" Dorothy teased.

"Oh, that was just a trick!" Stevie said, embarrassed that Dorothy had overheard her.

"But it was a clever one," Dorothy said, overtaking the girls from the rear. "And, besides, Max tells me you're showing a lot of promise in dressage, and you must know that a lot of that is just tricks, too."

"Sure, but dressage 'tricks,' as you call them, are *hard* tricks," Stevie said. "With Comanche, when you want him to talk, all you've got to do is to tickle him under his chin!"

"And then think of what you want him to say," Dorothy reminded her. "It was very entertaining—and the only time I've ever known a riding demonstration to be funny."

Stevie smiled. She was pleased by Dorothy's attention, and, for once, she didn't know what to say.

"This has been great!" Carole said, coming to Stevie's aid. "It was neat of you to come visit us. I wish we could see you ride some more."

"I'm sorry I can't stay, Carole. I'd love to spend more time with you girls. But I've got to get back to New York now. The American Horse Show is coming up soon and I've got work to do before that. See, my old teacher,

Max, has high expectations of me, so I've got to be in top form."

"I'm sure you'll win all kinds of ribbons in the show," Carole said. "You always do, don't you?"

"I've been lucky," Dorothy said, smiling. "Hard to tell how long my kind of luck runs. In the meantime, you girls keep working. You've got a wonderful start—and there's no better teacher, anywhere, you know?"

"We know," Lisa said. "We just don't want *him* to know."

"Know what?" Max asked, returning from the ring where he'd been greeting the stable's guests.

"Oh, nothing, Max," Dorothy said airily. "It's just one of your old students comparing notes with your new ones."

The four students, old and new, exchanged smiles.

Max knew better than to ask again. "Dorothy, I think you ought to untack your horse now," he said.

"Chores," Dorothy said. "Even after all these years, he's still bossing me around!"

The girls laughed. "See, the silly season," Stevie whispered.

"That's just Max," Carole said aloud.

"I wouldn't want him to change," Dorothy said.

"Not much," Stevie said, wiggling her eyebrows.

Max and Dorothy turned to the task of untacking her horse and putting him back in the horse trailer.

The girls still had some work to do with their own

horses. They'd planned a Saddle Club stop at TD's before going to Carole's house for their sleepover. They scurried around the stalls, untacking and grooming their horses, then rushed to get their knapsacks in the locker area. They were all anxious to get going.

There was an awful lot to talk about!

About the Author

Bonnie Bryant is the author of nearly a hundred books about horses, including the Saddle Club series, the Saddle Club Super Editions, and the Pony Tales series.